M

W

Praise for Jennifer Paddock
A Secret Word

"*A Secret Word* is a remarkably subtle and n

novel, which captures the dreamy rhythms of

staccato moments of c

memorable young sou

inexorably into the cosr

many first novelists wav

attention, Jennifer Pad   ...e reader with the narrative

equivalent of a raised e, SPow or the almost imperceptible nod of

the head. At the end the reader is inclined to ask of the writer as

well as her characters—what's next?"

> —Jay McInerney, author of *Bright Lights, Big City*

"Striking . . . a subtle, surprising first novel, with unforgettable
characters, a quiet sense of place and a nuanced exploration of the
secrets, loves, despairs, friends, and relatives that shape our lives."

> —*Publishers Weekly*

"[An] uncommonly assured debut . . . Paddock's narrative is decep-
tively simple. Her characters neither implausibly obsess over minu-
tiae nor have conveniently placed dramatic episodes; instead, their
creator relies on a smoothly authoritative voice to simply carry us
through. An unusually generous spirit animates these pages,
knowledgeable about shared pain, the call of the big city, disap-
pointments, and secret keeping. . . . the lucky discovery of three
secret diaries."

> —*Kirkus Reviews*

"*A Secret Word* is a rare gem of a book, distilled and heartbreaking, yet full of quiet grace that illuminates the page in extraordinary ways. There is something about Paddock's writing that defies conventional description. The closest word I can summon is 'magic.'"

—Melinda Haynes, author of *Mother of Pearl*

"Written with grace and insight, it is a remarkable first outing for this author."

—*Tucson Citizen*

"An ambitious novel with a fresh and original narrative . . . powerful. Paddock skillfully connects the chapters with distinctly unique voices . . . reveals each character's emotional state at different points in their lives. The reader is left with an exciting sense of voyeurism—like getting a secret glimpse into someone's life every few years and witnessing the powerful consequences of their reality at that moment. The effect leaves us understanding them on a deep level; we care about what happens to them."

—*Jackson Free Press*

"Jennifer Paddock has written a perfect novel-in-stories. *A Secret Word* is whole in a way that most of the kind are not; it resonates. That's partly because the three women at the center of the story are so memorable, their lives so inexorably linked, and partly because Paddock writes like Raymond Carver with a bigger heart—simple, graceful but tough, always with an eye on the possibility of redemption."

—Michael Knight, author of *Goodnight, Nobody*

"A subtle and moving insight into burgeoning adulthood."

—*Ellegirl* (UK)

ALSO BY JENNIFER PADDOCK

A Secret Word

POINT CLEAR

JENNIFER
PADDOCK

A Touchstone Book
Published by Simon & Schuster
New York   London   Toronto   Sydney

TOUCHSTONE
Rockefeller Center
1230 Avenue of the Americas
New York, NY 10020

TOUCHSTONE and colophon are registered trademarks
of Simon & Schuster, Inc.

For information regarding special discounts for bulk purchases,
please contact Simon & Schuster Special Sales at 1-800-456-6798
or business@simonandschuster.com.

Designed by Sarah Maya Gubkin

Manufactured in the United States of America

10   9   8   7   6   5   4   3   2   1

Library of Congress Cataloging-in-Publication Data
  Paddock, Jennifer.
    Point Clear / Jennifer Paddock.
      p.   cm.
    1. Women novelists—Fiction. 2. Missing persons—Fiction. 3.
    Swimmers—Fiction. 4. Alabama—Fiction. I. Title
  PS3616.A3355P65 2006
  813'.6—dc22   2006040939

ISBN-13: 978-0-7432-8782-1
ISBN-10:   0-7432-8782-7

For Sidney

CONTENTS

Part Four

Part Five

It seems to me that man's inclination toward light, toward brightness, is very nearly botanical—and I mean spiritual light. One not only needs it, one struggles for it.

—JOHN CHEEVER

PART
ONE

1. | SPINNING

On the sidewalks across Manhattan, especially in the morning, everyone moved with the appearance of direction. Caroline thought that they were probably all as lost as she was. They were empty and unanchored, so they were swift. No one Caroline knew was an exception.

Caroline's boss Rita, who was fifty, loved saying that she was exactly where she wanted to be in life. She was a famous restaurant critic, had a fabulous boyfriend, and had to pay only five hundred dollars a month for a rent-controlled apartment on the Upper West Side. That's where Caroline had worked with Rita for the past four months. And today was Caroline's last day.

The last time she'd nod to the doorman and agree with him about the weather. The last time she'd close her eyes and ride the slow old elevator up. The building in its decay had once seemed glamorous, and so had the job, and so had Rita. But as soon as Caroline opened the door and saw Rita with a personal trainer, both jogging in place and wearing leotards, Caroline knew she was right to leave.

"Make a dinner reservation at Ruby Foo's on Seventy-seventh for tonight at eight," Rita shouted at Caroline, and Caroline hurried to her desk to take notes.

"But use *your* name," Rita said, without pausing in her workout, still shouting to be heard over the constant encouragement of her personal trainer, whom Caroline had never seen before but who looked a lot like Rita's other middle-aged discount personal trainers—with bangs and long wavy hair and a slow, hippielike voice. *That's it, Rita. You got it. Both arms. Keep it moving. Now, don't forget to breathe. March. March. Feel strong. Beautiful.*

Caroline held her head steady, reminding herself not to look up. *Forget their flailing just inches away. Don't suddenly tilt your ears and get dizzy. Feel strong. Beautiful.*

"Use your phone number, too," said Rita, and Caroline imagined Rita out with Joel Grey and her other celebrity friends, saying, "Four for Caroline Berry." Rita could never use her own name. Sometimes she even wore a hat or sunglasses.

"And can you return that umbrella for me to the Italian umbrella store on Columbus and either Eighty-seventh or Eighty-eighth?"

Caroline glanced up without moving her head, reminding herself of how her doctor described her condition. Vertigo was merely the hallucination of motion. When she suffered from it, she was really steady, really still, she wasn't really spinning.

"I got it for a gift," said Rita, pointing toward the corner of the room where there were old bent cardboard boxes, rolls of new wrapping paper, several used bows, and a tall, pale blue umbrella with gold stitching, "but it broke."

Caroline studied the umbrella from a distance, and from

there it looked to be covered in quite a bit of dust and possibly crumbs from an old muffin. It had been standing in the corner with those boxes and wrapping paper since the first day she walked in, so she couldn't imagine anyone wanting or *trying* to take it back, and now she would have to herself. She wished she were in Alabama already. "A strange place to want to go," her friend Emma had said. But it wasn't to Caroline. She'd heard about it her whole life.

"An exchange will be fine," Rita said, stretching side to side. *Work the waistline. You can do it.*

A month ago, Caroline's mother had called her with news that her grandfather, her father's father, had died. It had reminded her of another call she had gotten from her mother, at the start of her freshman year in college, nine years ago, when her father was killed in a car wreck. But this call didn't have the same sadness or urgency. Her grandfather had died at ninety-three. "I understand if you can't make the funeral, being so far away, up there in New York," her mother told her, "but it would be nice if you could."

Later that afternoon, she had met Emma in Union Square and talked about what she should do. Emma said, "I wouldn't think of missing it because I'm so close with my family." That was when Caroline's vision began blurring and everything started spinning—all of Union Square, the storefronts, the taxis, the trees, the running dogs in the dog run, the water towers on roofs, the clouded sky, the digital clock on the art wall with the long line of fast and slow and frenzied yellow numbers—and Emma helped her cross the street back to Caroline's building. They made it to the door before Caroline threw up in the entry-way, and Emma was saying, "That's okay, you're okay, let's get you in bed," because Caroline couldn't stand on her own. Emma stood next to the bed, shifting a trash can back and forth, trying to catch Caroline's vomit. "Don't move, don't move," Caroline said, not realizing that she was the one who was moving because her eyes were moving in one direction and jumping quickly back to the opposite direction. "Oh, your eyes," Emma said. "I'm calling an ambulance." Paramedics came and strapped her onto a stretcher, and Caroline was afraid she was going to die in the elevator and then in the ambulance.

At the emergency room, she was given something to calm her and the movement of her eyes and something for nausea. She had an MRI to make sure there wasn't an acoustic neuroma, a brain tumor. But there was no tumor. Nothing was seriously wrong. The doctor finally diagnosed her condition as vertigo and suspected the sudden appearance of it was stress-related. She was given meclizine, which made her feel as if her head had been filled with cement and couldn't be moved. And she didn't believe she could move or should move. So there was no choice about flying home for her grandfather's funeral. She stayed where she was, as long as she could, in a private room in Saint Vincent's hospital. For three days, she lived with around-the-clock I.V.s, a kind nurse, a television positioned perfectly, and the most beautiful window view of the city, which never moved once. She cried when she left that room.

When Caroline said goodbye to Rita at noon, Rita was on the phone but gave her the check for the week, then waved and said hoarsely, from so much shouting, "Did you write down everything you've been doing for the next person?" Rita had been through this many times before. Three assistants already this year.

Caroline nodded and shut the door. Walking to the elevator, some of the heaviness she had been feeling lately left her. Outside on Broadway, where it was bright and slightly cool for early September, she felt even better. Free from the first of her two jobs. Free at last from Rita. Free from having to take Rita's dry cleaning and pick it up every week at the New York School of Dry Cleaning thirty blocks away just so Rita could save a little money. Then Caroline remembered why she was carrying the umbrella and walked toward the subway.

To her astonishment, the umbrella store, a small boutique that specialized in umbrellas and parasols in silk and cotton (one was even trimmed in mink), took the return and gave Caroline a similar $245 umbrella in exchange. Caroline went back to the subway and found herself using the umbrella as a cane as she went down the steps. This reminded her of how her brother, Casey, when they were young and still close—before their father died—broke a bone in his foot by jumping off the house, and instead of using crutches he used a cane, because he thought it would be cooler.

Instead of going back up to Rita's office and having to say goodbye again, she left the umbrella with the doorman, then decided to take a cab to her next job—walking down the subway stairs again seemed like such an ordeal. The cab would cost ten dollars, but she would get the drive through Central Park. Lately, and more and more frequently, Caroline tried to remember that the city didn't only wear you down every day but could uplift you and save you. A cab ride through Central Park could save you. There were beauty and silence in the trees, but also through them were flickering lights and scattered noise, Manhattan itself, alive.

After she got out of the cab on East Thirty-sixth, before going into the tall black-granite building with the green awning where she worked as an assistant to a literary agent, she stopped at the newsstand for a *New York Post*. She liked to read the gossip on Page Six.

She paid for the paper and reached for a Nutter Butter, then thought better of it and put it back. "Take it," the guy said and winked at her, so she did.

When she walked into the agent's office on the twenty-first floor, which was cramped and messy but with a clear view of the Empire State Building, she was greeted with a long, warm "Hello, Caroline."

"Hi, Miriam," she said, smiling at the sight of Miriam dressed up more than usual, wearing a loose-hanging black dress with bright pink flowers, while on the floor next to her were her worn-out, faded black heels, apparently kicked off, and tangled black hose, pulled inside out.

"I had a breakfast date," Miriam said, explaining her outfit. "And now I'm going to order us lunch. A farewell lunch," she said, even though she ordered lunch for them every day. "What would you like? A cheeseburger? Pizza? Chinese?"

"A cheeseburger sounds fun. And I just got a free Nutter Butter," said Caroline, opening her purse to show her. "The newsstand guy gave it to me."

Miriam let a silence between them lengthen. "You know, I used to be young and blond, too. I wasn't always like this."

Caroline didn't know what to say, so she just nodded, then said, "I know," though it was hard for her to imagine.

"Okay," Miriam said and dialed the number for Sarge's Deli. "I'd like two cheeseburger deluxes, two sixteen-ounce-bottle Cokes, two cups of ice." She looked over to Caroline for her approval.

Caroline gave her a thumbs-up. They were very similar people, both messy with bad eating habits, both single and on their own in Manhattan, though they had much different backgrounds. Miriam was seventy and had grown up in the city just a few blocks away and gone to City College. She had started out as an assistant, and then later started her own agency.

Everyone she represented was a quality writer, including a Nobel Prize winner and a Pulitzer Prize winner. She was not a writer, though, not like Caroline hoped to be.

Caroline was twenty-seven, had grown up in Tulsa, and majored in English at the University of Tulsa, doing her best in creative writing. In fiction workshops, teachers praised her, boys developed crushes on her. When she was accepted into NYU's graduate creative writing program and rented her own apartment in Manhattan, she felt elated, and for a while she believed she could become a writer, but at NYU she lost confidence. In class, she felt almost invisible, a ghost, and she knew she was not alone in this feeling. Most people in New York seemed like ghosts.

Caroline only had about seventy pages of short stories, her thesis. "I can tell you're good," Miriam had said. But Miriam hadn't read anything that Caroline had written. Miriam didn't really read anyone's work anymore. She just memorized a line, and then recited it back to the author. "It makes them so happy," she once explained. "And it's so easy to do."

Caroline got settled into her desk. Miriam liked for her to sit at the bigger desk with the computer. When Caroline looked over at her, Miriam was looking back.

"When you get back from your writing sabbatical to Alabama, you could work here again. We'll send out your novel."

"Thanks, Miriam," Caroline said, trying to smile, but there was no way she was going to return to either of her jobs or be able to write a novel in three weeks. When she had given her two-week notice, Miriam had kept prodding her about what in the world she would do with herself in Alabama for three whole weeks, and Caroline had made the mistake of saying she might try to do a little writing. *Might. Try.* Ultimately, Miriam didn't think writing was something that difficult, if you were a writer.

But it was nice that Miriam wanted her to return. After working for four years with her, Caroline had become the closest thing Miriam had to family, and Miriam may have been the closest thing that Caroline had, too. It seemed that way, at least. Her father was dead, she never saw her one brother, and now her mother was remarried and was always traveling all over the world (though never to New York) with her new husband. When Caroline went home to Tulsa, her mother had napkins from Brussels, a bookmark from Dublin, a carved wooden statue from somewhere in Africa. Her mother had been on a safari, slept outside. "You have to be careful where you eat," her mother had said.

The doorbell rang. The doorman always let Sarge's right up.

Miriam raised her hands and swayed as if she were dancing in her chair. "The cheeseburgers!" she said, and began to clear a space on her desk, while Caroline answered the door and paid by signing Miriam's name on the credit-card receipt.

After Caroline divvied up the food and drinks and ketchup and mustard packages, she went to get her *Post*, since Miriam had her *Publishers Weekly*.

They were usually quiet while they ate, though this time Caroline didn't really read. She couldn't focus. She thought about how this was their last meal together and how she was not coming back, how after her trip she could leave New York altogether. If she wanted to, she could pack and leave in one day. She had arrived in New York with only clothes and a few books, and she hadn't acquired much furniture—only a bed, desk, bookcase, and kitchen table with two chairs that a neighbor moving out had given her.

Caroline had inherited enough money from her grandfather to afford a three-week trip to Alabama. There she would decide what her next step in life should be. She knew her grandfather would approve, that it would almost seem as if he were going with her, since it was his money that was taking her and since he had been the one who first discovered the Grand Hotel in Point Clear, Alabama, where he made yearly visits to play golf.

Her parents had stayed at the Grand Hotel for their honeymoon, and countless times throughout her life she had heard them tell about the 550-acre antebellum resort, about the three-hundred-year-old live oaks, the Spanish moss, the magnolias, the longleaf pines, the palms, the red, yellow, purple, pink, any-color-you-can-imagine flowers, and the brackish, shallow water of Mobile Bay, but she had never been.

After they finished lunch, Miriam surprised her by saying she didn't have any fieldwork, which is what she called it when Caroline had to go outside and run errands. Caroline had figured that since it was her last day and Miriam didn't like to go out herself, she would at least have to go to the bank or to Kinko's. Instead, she soaked the unused stamps off of return envelopes from author submissions, wrote a few cover letters, sent a few e-mails, and whenever the phone rang, she said Miriam was at lunch, or in a meeting, or on the other line. Then, at the end of the day, Miriam did something she had never done—she called her car service to take Caroline home.

"And here," she said, giving Caroline two checks, one that was her regular pay and one that was for three hundred dollars. "A bonus," she said.

"Thank you, Miriam," Caroline said. She put the checks in the side pocket of her purse, and Miriam followed her to the door.

"Call me when you get back," she said, "if you want to."

Then she widened her eyes, looking hopeful that Caroline would return. Caroline knew Miriam didn't want to hire a new assistant. Miriam had once said, with a look of horror, "Now you know all my secrets."

Caroline put an arm around her. Miriam, especially with her shoes off, was much shorter than Caroline, and as Miriam looked up at her, Caroline felt a true fondness pass between them. "Bye, Miriam," she said.

The ride in the car service should have been relaxing, but the driver was listening to Indian techno with an electric sitar wailing over an insistent disco drum machine, and Park Avenue was dirtier than she'd ever seen it, with bags of trash piled like hedges along the curbs, litter blowing by on the sidewalk and street. When she first moved to New York, before 9/11, the city was much cleaner, but now, and more and more often, it was as if there were a permanent garbage strike.

She curled her hand absently over her mouth, thinking about what she needed to do before her flight tomorrow morning. She still had to pack and clean up her apartment for Emma, who would be staying there while she was away. Emma was her best friend from NYU, a film student who still hadn't graduated, taking only one course a semester, while living at home with her parents in New Jersey.

Before Union Square, the driver turned left on Eighteenth, then right on Irving Place, as if he had driven her home before and knew the quickest route to her apartment on Fifteenth.

"Thanks," she said and shut the door, and as the driver pulled away, she was already thinking again about what to pack and hoping the washing machines were open in the basement when she saw Emma leaning against the front of her building. Tall, blond, pretty, and smoking, like always.

Emma saw her and dramatically stubbed out her cigarette

on one of the four marble pillars in front of the building, then immediately dug into her purse for another one and lit it. "I'm sorry I'm already here," she said, flashing silver from a stud in her tongue. She had a lot of luggage at her feet. "I had to get out. It's my sisters, my mother, my father. And then there's Anthony."

"It's always about Anthony," Caroline said. Anthony was a man whom Emma had been having an affair with, and he was married with kids. Anthony could only see well out of one eye and was not a good driver. Emma sometimes called him "One-eye Anthony."

"It's okay," Caroline said and grabbed one of her bags, a duffel bag that was so crammed full of clothes it couldn't be zipped up. Caroline showed her which key fit the outside door, and Emma watched as Caroline stood on her toes, pushing the key in and up to turn the lock.

In the lobby, Emma gazed at the thin, winding staircase that went up twelve floors. "This would make a great shot for my short film." Emma loved Alfred Hitchcock. People had told her that she looked like Kim Novak. "Anybody'd get vertigo staring up there. Maybe that's all it is, maybe you just have to stop looking at this."

Caroline stared at the floor, marble with cracks. "I don't look at the stairs, ever. I did when I first moved here, but now, never." And tomorrow on her flight, she thought, she might peer for a second out a window, but she would do so from an aisle seat.

As they took the elevator up to the ninth floor, Caroline noticed that the rest of Emma's bags were not bags but black film-equipment cases. Emma caught her eyeing them. "Is it still all right if I shoot in your apartment and maybe get an exterior of your building and a quick shot of the foyer?"

"Just be careful," Caroline said, imagining Emma carting up her whole heap of film gear—the lenses and lights and C-stands, clunky, heavy metal things that stuck out everywhere. "I'm pretty sure I'm supposed to get permission from the co-op board, and I haven't."

"Oh, definitely," Emma said. "I can be sneaky."

Before opening the apartment door, Caroline showed her which key on the ring fit, then as they walked in, they had to weave through clothes strewn around the floor and two Sunday *New York Times* that needed to be taken to the basement for recycling.

"Don't worry," Caroline said, "I'll clean up tonight."

"You don't need to clean up for me," Emma said. "I'll feel right at home here."

"No, no," Caroline said, looking around, trying to decide where to begin, and she felt her head jerk, and the floor became uneven. She closed her eyes, telling herself it was only a hallucination, then she steadied herself. Emma didn't notice. She was leaning out the kitchen window to see the full view of Union Square Park.

When Caroline looked back on her life, she could see signs of vertigo. As a kid, she'd fainted twice, once when she lost a tooth and another time when she was baptized. When she finished grad school and was searching for full-time work, she became dizzy at an interview at a talent agency, where she failed the typing test, then again after an interview for a newsmagazine, where she was told that there wasn't anything open at the moment, but if there ever was they'd give her a call. As she was walking out the door, the head of the fact-checking department added, "But one more thing, just so you know, we work through a temp office, so there are no benefits."

Great, she thought, might as well keep working for Miriam.

Then Emma said she could get her the job with Rita. Emma had once been Rita's assistant, but had had to quit because the commute from Jersey wasn't worth it, and parking was a problem. "Are you sure?" Emma had asked Caroline. "You know it's going to be awful. I mean it's kind of cool. It's a cool thing to say you work for her, but it's really very awful." So it was Miriam and Rita, and that was the best she thought she could do. But now she had to change. She had to take control. Her life couldn't keep spinning the way it was.

She looked at Emma still leaning out the window, studying her new view. Emma needed a different perspective as much as she did. *Three weeks away*. She and Emma shared this thought.

PART TWO

2. | POINT CLEAR

Landing in Mobile was much like landing in Tulsa or any other midsize city, but riding out of Mobile was like riding out of nowhere else Caroline had ever been: past a battleship in the harbor, then for miles crossing the bridge over Mobile Bay, the water around her a blinding yellow-white sheen, as if she were crossing the sun itself. Then seeing an alligator lying on the bank of a bayou. Then passing southward through towns each smaller than the last, and each growing more quaint, until she could not have been more eager to arrive at Point Clear.

The driver of the shuttle van spoke very little, as if he could detect that she was someone without someone to love, without much of a life, someone with no career whose family was dwindling—just a girl with a past—and knew she needed silence, to see every sailboat and every pier and every bay house hard to see and every catch of moss hanging from live oaks that canopied the last stretch of the drive that carried her to the heart of Point Clear, the Grand Hotel.

The hotel seemed grand already with its wrought-iron gate and the windy road on the other side, which led through more live oaks, which truly did look alive, with their gray limbs twisting and reaching over the road and over the duck pond and over the garden plots of flowers she couldn't name. "Now, that's a tree a boy can climb," her father would have said.

When the driver unloaded her bags from the back, he said that from the peninsula of Point Clear you could see the bay meet the gulf. Here was the place where her grandfather would come, she thought, where he wanted to be more than any place in the world.

After she checked in and found her room at the secluded end of one of the wings, she sat in a rocking chair on the balcony. She looked a long time at a fishing pier, then at the bay meeting the gulf, then at the sky.

She was glad to have this peace, this solitude, this environment so different from New York. Memories were coming to her here, charged with emotion and immediacy. Remembering what Miriam had called this break—"a writing sabbatical"—she retrieved her laptop.

Trying to write something. After my father died, my mother and I would go visit my grandfather and bring him lunch. He lived in Utica Square, the old part of town. His house was a white wooden two-story with black shutters, and there was a guesthouse in back. "That's where a maid used to live," my mother once told me, making her voice higher, with both awe and shame. But no one lived there then. He seemed so happy to see us, happy to have a Braum's hamburger, happy to have Long John Silver's fish. We'd go in the back way, and he'd let us in through a screen door. He always looked nice, his shirt ironed and tucked into dress pants, his loafers polished. There was a nurse that came in the morning to help him exercise, and I guess she helped him dress and cleaned the place up. He could walk okay, but he wasn't himself. He was so friendly and grateful, missing my father, his son. Before I had almost been afraid of him, and he'd almost been afraid of me.

My brother and I reacted so differently to our father's death. I was mostly just sad, I didn't say much, but Casey was angry, and was angry that I wasn't angry. He blamed Dad completely. Blamed him for wrecking his car and dying. Blamed him for losing his job at fifty as an oil executive, then for using his severance pay to buy an Alfa Romeo sports car. "Why would he even buy that car? Why couldn't he have been more careful in that car?" Casey said around the house in the days that seemed to drag on forever before the funeral.

Trying to remember what happened after my father died, as if it might tie together these events for a novel somehow, for someone like me at a beautiful *place like this missing her father like my father and her grandfather like my grandfather.*

Proud of her last line, she stopped and closed her laptop. For now, that was enough. Smiling, and breathing a little deeper here, she waited for sunset.

3. | THE YELLOW SHIRT

Maybe Caroline was living in the past. Maybe that was her problem.

It was sunny and felt like a hundred degrees outside, and not knowing how else to start her sabbatical at the Grand Hotel resort, she decided to walk around and see the place, her new home for three weeks; but she realized quickly that she did not have on the right clothes. She was wearing black pants, sandals, and a long-sleeved white linen shirt, which would have been all right for last night when she sat on the balcony, a breeze coming off the bay, but today the outfit was all wrong.

She really needed to be wearing shorts and a sleeveless top. She had packed a few pairs of shorts and shirts to play tennis in, but those were from high school, when she was still playing tennis all the time. In the summer in New York, she had taken a lesson from a Jamaican pro in Central Park, and he looked at her racquet, which was a Wilson Pro Staff, like what Pete Sampras used to play with, then at her clothes—Ellesse, even older, like what Chris Evert used to wear—and said, "You're living in the past, man." Walking around the grounds, walking where her grandfather and parents had walked years before, she knew he'd been right.

But she had bought a new Babolat racquet in New York, which she had with her. She should have bought new tennis clothes as well, but the place where she was shopping was crowded and there weren't any dressing rooms open at the time, so she hadn't. Probably even then she knew that she would want to buy something at the Grand Hotel that she could take home with her.

So now her walk around the hotel grounds had a purpose for the present—to buy new tennis clothes, perhaps even schedule a lesson.

Walking along the redbrick sidewalk by the bay, she passed a family playing croquet on the hotel lawn. She hadn't played since she was a kid, when she got a croquet set one Christmas. Another Christmas she got a badminton set. Her brother's gifts always seemed more interesting—a saltwater aquarium, a guitar, a tent with mesh windows that was big enough to stand in.

It seemed odd to look up and see so much space where so many buildings could be, and it seemed exotic when she saw a flock of pelicans soaring silently over her on their prehistoric wings.

She walked through a gate and saw an enormous pool, curved like a lagoon, with a rocky waterfall and some kind of area where the water bubbled and where everyone seemed to be gravitating, bobbing up and down, and also a smaller pool, the branches of a nearby live oak, with its hanging moss, shadowing one end. Since it was after Labor Day, both sides were mostly filled with adults, especially the two hot tubs between the pools. Married adults and retired adults. Not singles like her whom she might meet and get to know.

She decided to walk over to the spa building, which had a workout area that overlooked a marina, then she walked past the indoor pool, where New Age music was playing and there were platters of cookies, bowls of fruit, and tea. When she reached the balcony outside, she stood a moment and looked out at the sailboats and yachts and thought about how lucky she was to be there. Then she realized that she hadn't been dizzy once since she'd arrived. Maybe the fresh air was curing her.

She bounded down the steps and took a path along the marina, then crossed the road toward the tennis courts, and it was then she finally saw, across from the courts, her grandfather's golf course, which had a marsh and a footbridge and, in the distance, green hills, lakes, and trees that in the sun looked lacy. She thought she could smell pine and cedar, along with fertile earth.

Golf carts passed by and the people in them said hello to her, and she said hello back, which felt odd but fun to do, saying hello to strangers. Before she reached the tennis shop, she stopped and pulled her blouse away from her skin so she wouldn't look too sweaty.

The tennis shop reminded her of the one she went to growing up. It was about the size of a shack but was somewhat nice inside, with racquets on the wall, a stringing machine, and two round racks of clothes. She thought no one was there, but then a man appeared from the dressing room carrying a broad sword in both hands. "Can I help ya?" he said, with an Irish accent.

"Oh, no," she said, feeling flustered, not expecting the sword or the accent. "Well, yes, maybe. I'm just looking."

He smiled, then set his sword in the corner. He was tall and tan, in his late thirties, at least somewhat close to her age, and his eyes were very blue. "I'm Joseph," he said. "The tennis pro."

"Nice to meet you," she said and shook his hand. "I'm Caroline. I was wondering if I could schedule a lesson."

"Tomorrow at eleven would be magic," he said. "I just had a cancellation."

"Great," she said. She expected him to ask her how well she played, and she was looking forward to answering.

Instead, he looked over her head, which reminded her of being in a bar in New York, where often when a guy was talking to her, he'd look above her for someone better. "Magic," he said. "The Seagull's here."

She turned around to see a man who was closer to her own age, tan, with blondish-brown hair, in a yellow Nike shirt. He was carrying two Babolat racquets, like hers. His eyes were green like hers and lingered on her a moment, and she would normally have felt uneasy with someone so obviously attractive looking at her, but she felt calm, as if she could reach out and touch him and it would be the most natural thing in the world.

"He calls everyone the Seagull," the man said to her.

"Oh, no," the Irish tennis pro said, and swayed and waved an arm out for effect. "That's not true. Daniel is the Seagull. People will say you can't do this and you can't do that, but the Seagull wants to fly higher and faster than everyone else."

Daniel looked at her again, then back to Joseph. "Where's your sword?"

Joseph reached for it in the corner, slid it out of its sheath, then stabbed it into the Astroturf floor. "Dere's me sword!"

As they all watched the sword rock in place, an older woman wearing a pleated tennis skirt and gold-rimmed glasses on a chain walked in and sat behind the front desk. "All right," Joseph said in a professional way, then tucked his sword back into its sheath and the sheath under his arm. "Let's go."

Daniel turned to her and smiled, then followed Joseph outside.

"May I help you?" the woman said.

"I'm looking for a couple of outfits," Caroline said, then pulled pink shorts and a matching pink-and-gray top from the rack.

"Sure," the woman said. "The dressing room is behind you."

"Thanks," Caroline said, and grabbed a white skirt and tank top as well.

Caroline went into the dressing room and pushed the button lock, but she could see the woman through the shuttered door. "Are you on vacation?" the woman asked.

It seemed an odd time to be chatty. Caroline answered while she undressed. "Yes," she said. "From New York."

"We get a lot of people from New York."

"Really?" Caroline said, feeling somewhat disappointed.

"Oh, yeah," the woman said. "New York, New Jersey, Vermont."

Caroline looked at herself in the mirror. She was out of shape, but the clothes fit okay. Size eight for one outfit. Not bad. She had definitely been worse.

"The reason I ask, is, well, you do know about the hurricane? I just heard CNN and the *Today* show are coming to the hotel. And if they're coming, the hurricane's probably coming."

Caroline poked her head out of the door. "Hurricane?"

"If it stays on course, it'll make landfall in three or four days."

"Nobody told me at the front desk," Caroline said.

"Well, I guess they wouldn't," the woman said. "Don't worry. This hotel has been here almost two hundred years, through a lot of hurricanes. Frederick. Danny. Georges. And anyway, you can outrun a hurricane."

Caroline changed back to her own clothes, charged the outfits, then began to hurry back to her room to watch the weather on CNN. Then she remembered. She turned around, and though the court was partially blocked by a longleaf pine, she saw Daniel in the distance. She had been to the U.S. Open and had studied the players. Daniel had to be a professional player. It was evident in his balance and movement, which looked effortless. His swing flew above his shoulder, and his yellow shirt fluttered.

4. | WHAT COULD SHE DO?

Regardless of the channel, Caroline heard the same news: Hurricane Ivan was cutting a deadly swath through the Caribbean and was on a course for Alabama, with the eye apparently aimed directly at Point Clear. It was always possible Ivan could lose strength, but it was running a steady Category Four, and three times before it had sped up to Five. Other than stay informed, Caroline didn't know what to do. What could she do? Buy batteries and candles? Stock up on ice, nonperishables, and bottled water? Board up her windows? Store away any loose bricks or flowerpots in her yard that could become dangerous airborne debris? Be ready when word came from the governor to evacuate? None of the advice on television was directed to someone in her position, so she did the only logical thing: She did what everyone else at the hotel seemed to be doing: enjoying the hotel. So she changed into her bathing suit and went swimming.

First in the lagoonlike pool. She waded in and sat on the

steps, then went underwater. She had never properly learned how to swim freestyle, or breaststroke, or backstroke, or butterfly. She'd spent her childhood playing tennis at the expense, it seemed sometimes, of everything else. So she swam mostly, and best, underwater, where she thought no one could see her swim, or see her clearly. So she swam underwater, a few arm lengths at a time, off and on, until she decided to float on her back instead, because she floated with surprising authority, and because the bubble area, which made floating even easier, was too tempting to neglect.

Everything was too tempting to neglect. She made her way to the waterfall and stood beneath it until the crashing water began to sting her head and shoulders. So she swam underwater, took a breath, then swam underwater again, and eventually reached the shallow end, which was as shallow as a puddle but had fountains like geysers shooting up from the floor, which she imagined were for toddlers to run through. She walked through them on her way to the waterslide, which she went down once, and she felt brave, but once was enough.

What else was there to do? So she moved to the adult area, ordered a club sandwich from the snack bar, and ate it by the pool. What else was there to do now? She had brought *The Stories of John Cheever* with her, a paperback she had taken from her mother's house before moving to New York (she remembered her father mistakenly calling it *The Stories of John Heever* because of the big, separated *C*), so she lay in the shade to read for a while. But she couldn't concentrate, so she stopped, ordered a strawberry daiquiri, then drank it while sitting in the hot tub, while admiring the palm trees, the bamboo brakes, the live oaks, wondering if they would soon all be destroyed.

She spent the rest of the day in nervous anticipation, watching television in her room. Ivan was the most powerful hurricane to hit the Caribbean in ten years. Sixty-seven lives had been claimed so far. On the island of Grenada, ninety percent of the homes had been damaged. She saw the stats, she saw the footage of destruction, but she wasn't going anywhere, at least not yet. The hurricane could always change its course, so why should she change hers? Anyway, if the governor issued a mandatory evacuation, it wouldn't really be mandatory, as she had heard it explained, but merely advised. She had a tennis lesson scheduled for tomorrow, and she looked forward to it.

Before turning out the lights for the night, she took one of her dizzy pills, and from how she saw herself take it—with the same ginger placement of the pill on the tip of the tongue, then the same jerk of the head, everything, the two sips of water in succession, just like her father taking a pill—a surge of sorrow and loneliness and fear overtook her, and she suddenly sobbed, hard, uncontrollably.

When the tears slowed and she thought she could speak through them, she reached for the phone to call her mother.

Her mother sounded frightened when she answered. "Mom," Caroline said. "Are you all right?"

"Oh, I'm sorry. I was just asleep." Caroline could hear her mother getting situated, could imagine her propping up her pillow to talk in bed.

"I was just feeling blue, thinking about Dad."

"That's funny. I just had a dream about your father. Maybe because of where you are. You are there, aren't you?"

"I'm here. It's really lovely."

"That's good," her mother said. "I'm glad."

"What were you dreaming about?" Caroline asked.

"What I always dream when I dream about your father— that he is still alive, but he's living with a new woman. And I'm like I am today, married to David, but I am jealous and mad. Isn't that crazy?"

"I always dream that he's alive but he's going to die," Caroline said. "That he tells me he's going to die."

"Oh, Caroline. Let's not talk about this. Tell me about your room. Do you have a view? And have you played tennis? You know, tennis is what makes you the happiest. You were such a happy child."

Caroline carried the phone as far as she could toward the balcony, so she could look out at the water. "Haven't you seen the news about the hurricane?"

"I haven't," her mother said.

"Well, it's coming right for me."

"It is? Well, what are you going to do?"

"I don't know," Caroline said, and then she carried the phone back to the bedside table and got back into bed. "Stay, I guess. Or maybe leave."

"Well, David just walked in. Let's hang up now. Whatever you decide, be careful."

When Caroline got off the phone, she started to cry again and wished she hadn't even called. She supposed she wanted her mother to act like a mother and tell her to leave. To leave right then. So Caroline decided it was final, she would definitely, defiantly stay, and if she did die in the storm, her mother could dream guilt for a change, instead of always jealousy.

5. | STEEL SHUTTERS

Caroline's second morning in Point Clear began much like her first: awakened by the knock of room service, then breakfast on the balcony. The day was sunny.

After a long, relaxing shower, she put on her new pink-and-gray outfit, then grabbed her racquet. If she hurried, she wouldn't be late for her lesson.

Joseph was waiting on the court with his sword and a shopping cart of balls.

"What's that sword for?" she asked.

"It's me William Wallace sword," he said. "A tennis racquet's a sword, you know. It's your weapon. Because every match is like going to battle. You always come prepared to play, and you look at your opponent like they have a sword in their hands, too. So you can't be thinking about what happened yesterday, the fight with your brother or your boyfriend, or that you blew the last point. You've got to play in the moment, *every* moment—tennis is an existential sport. If you don't," he said, swinging the sword high above his shoulder, "I'm just going to cleave ye head off."

She laughed, and he seemed glad for the response, as if he knew he could teach her. He laid the sword in the shopping cart and took up his racquet. "I'll just feed you a few first and see how you play," he said. "Let's get you nice and loose here."

Caroline missed the first few, but then began to concentrate and get into a rhythm until she was playing like she played as a teenager. "Beautiful," Joseph said. "But I want to talk to you. Have you seen Maria Sharapova play?"

She nodded. He named other Russian women who played, mostly names she hadn't heard, then showed her how they hit their forehand and backhand, with a big follow-through, which Caroline thought she had been doing. He made her swing practice swings for him until she finally got it, but her shoulder began to hurt.

"Don't worry. You must have been taught fifteen, twenty years ago. But you can learn. You're too talented not to. Everything's different now. The game's changing."

He then taught her a shot called a forehand buggy whip, which required her to swing the racquet over her head, which she never quite got, even though he took out his sword and waved it in the air in an attempt to threaten and inspire her; so he moved on to a slice backhand, which she could do when he fed the ball perfectly to her, but she could never imagine doing it in a match.

They took several water breaks during the hour lesson, and he told her that Daniel was from Point Clear, that he was closing in on the top hundred in the world, and that he had flown out this morning to play in a tournament in Delray Beach, near Miami. Then he told her about himself, how he came to America to play in college, then played on the pro tour, but stopped after only two years because he fell in love. He was married and had a daughter.

Caroline didn't believe she had ever been in love, not really.

She'd only had one relationship in New York, with a medical student, and that lasted a year. Their relationship never felt as intense and heightened as it should have. She always knew she wasn't going to stay with him, even when he would talk about marriage, and the breakup had been easy. She missed talking to him, though. He would listen to her talk about her father. He told her once that it took four years for a person to move on after a death, but Caroline didn't believe you ever really moved on. The death of someone you loved would always color everything.

Caroline hoped that her actions in college were really just grieving. Her first year in the dorm, she hooked up with a man ten years older and lived with him. Later, she told her mother that she only did so to get out of the dorm, but the truth was that she thought she loved him. He was an alcoholic and a gambling addict and often was mean to her, but he was funny and smart. Caroline forced herself to get over him and moved into a house with three roommates. For the next three years in that house, with roommates coming in and out, she drank, smoked cigarettes and pot, tried opium, Ecstasy, and LSD, had regular prescriptions of Ambien and Xanax. She kissed strange boys at parties, slept with one whose name she didn't remember. By the time she got to New York, she was partied out and had become a very respectable social drinker. Sometimes she didn't drink at all and would have a Sprite, which looked like a gin and tonic. She was drug-free, except for the meclizine, which she could buy over the counter. And she never smoked. She hoped Emma was at least smoking out the kitchen window in her apartment.

At the end of the lesson, Joseph told her that he would soon be spinning at the hotel bar on Friday nights and she must come. She thought at first "spinning" had something to do with Irish river dancing, but what he meant, she realized, was that he was going to be a DJ, spinning records. "It'll be called Celtic

Twilight Hour," he said, and Caroline said the name had a nice ring to it. "And if the Seagull's in town, he'll be there," he said. She hoped he might mean something by this, but she didn't ask. She didn't want to hear if Daniel was married with a kid, too, or if he had a girlfriend.

Joseph motioned for her to follow him to the tennis pro shop. The woman who had worked at the front desk yesterday was gone, and Joseph went behind the desk and unzipped a gym bag lying on the floor that was filled with hundreds of CDs without their cases. "You might want to clean it first," he said, and gave her a CD by a band she'd never heard of: the Waterboys. "This is savage," he said, and told her that the first song was really a Yeats poem put to music, and then he recited four lines. Caroline told him that she was a writer, or at least that she went to school for writing. And he told her that he was one, too. He wrote poetry and children's books.

"I can read you something if you have any time," he said.

"Okay, sure," she said.

He set a chair out for her, and then reached back into his gym bag. He dug through the CDs until he found sheets of notebook paper that looked like they had been folded and refolded many times, then proceeded to read her a story that was dedicated to his daughter. He read with passion, and his accent seemed to get thicker, every "th" sound replaced with a "d." Caroline was having trouble understanding him and following the plot. Something about a white light dat would let ships know dey had reached da west coast of Ireland. Treacherous cliffs and black rocks. A fairy. There was a little girl, whose name was also his daughter's name, saving her parents. Caroline nodded along, trying to smile when she was supposed to, but she was exhausted from the tennis lesson. When he came to the final page, a corner at the top had been torn away, and he looked for it, but it was missing, so he just skipped the lines and told her what was happening.

When he finished, she sat a little straighter and told him she really liked it, that it really was good.

"Ah," he said, shaking his head and starting to fold up the pages, "I could tell ye were bored."

"No, no," she said. "I really liked it." What she wanted to say was that she was impressed that he could read his work like that in front of her. That he was a writer more than she was. What she said instead was, "Are you leaving for the hurricane?"

"No," he said, stuffing the pages back into his gym bag and zipping it up. "We're staying. My wife has horses. She won't leave them. We've got a brick house, and I'll board me windows. What're you going to do?"

She paused because she was tempted to tell him the truth, then thought better of it and shrugged. "I'll do whatever the hotel tells me," she said.

Caroline said goodbye and walked back toward the hotel, and as she passed the spa building, she saw office workers wheeling dollies loaded with office files into a van. She decided to go inside, and the women who worked in the salon were clearing out the little shop where they sold bath products and yoga clothes. Caroline asked if they expected the hotel to be destroyed, and the oldest one, with red hair and a name tag that read MANAGER, said, "Not really, hon. It's the storm surge we're concerned with the most, the possible flooding. We've got to move everything out."

Caroline nodded, then took the exit facing the marina. Many of the boats she'd seen yesterday—including all the yachts—were gone, and those few that remained were buckled down tight, with their masts lowered and the cabins covered with tarps. She followed the brick path along the bay and spotted the satellite dishes of two broadcasting trucks parked in the lot. CABLE NEWS NETWORK, INC. was printed in simple black letters on the driver's side door of the larger truck. The smaller one wasn't marked, but she guessed it belonged to the *Today* show. This was exciting to Caroline, but she didn't know why. She had never had any remote interest in joining the crowd that collected every morning in Rockefeller Center to see a live broadcast of the *Today* show. It seemed like a silly thing to do in New York if you lived in New York. She never peered through the glass of the CNN studio on Sixth Avenue, though she'd passed it numerous times. But here in Alabama, where you never expected news to be, it suddenly seemed thrilling, and she couldn't wait to get to her room to see Point Clear on the national news.

All along the way to the far side of the building where she was staying, she watched hotel workers making preparations for the hurricane. The pool employees were putting away umbrellas and submerging all the deck chairs and tables into the pools, and groundskeepers were hanging steel shutters over the restaurant windows. She crossed the empty lawn where croquet had been played yesterday and asked one of the groundskeepers what they were planning to do about the sliding-glass doors to all the rooms.

"Nothing," he said, then shook his head. "But I wouldn't worry too much yet. It's still way out in the gulf."

Caroline smiled and stepped away, then stopped to watch a pelican in free fall, with its beak only slightly open and its wings forked back in a W. She was mesmerized by how pelicans turned from their graceful flight to drop downward and rush crashing into the water beak first, then bobbed up unhurt, which seemed miraculous, and if they'd caught the fish they sought, as this one had, they'd lift their beaks and throw their heads back, just like Caroline or her father taking a pill. To that

pelican, or to those other pelicans resting on pier posts or glid-
ing overhead, or to that blue heron standing on the rocks of a
jetty, or to those seagulls scattered along the beach, a hurricane
wasn't coming. There was nothing but the present. Caroline
thought it was a fine way to live.

In her room, the message light on her phone was flashing.
It was a message from the front desk to all hotel guests,
announcing that since Hurricane Ivan was projected to make
landfall in three days, there was a mandatory evacuation order.
Everyone would have to check out of their rooms by noon
tomorrow, or preferably earlier, and if anyone needed a ride to
the airport, shuttles would be available.

She hung up, then reached for the remote. CNN wasn't
broadcasting from Point Clear yet, so she switched to other
channels and found one out of Mobile that was showing live
coverage of the nearby town of Fairhope, which she remembered driving through because of all the flowers set around
town, even potted on the tops of trash cans. The flowers, thou-
sands of them, were now being removed and loaded onto
flatbed trucks for safekeeping in nurseries. Patients at local
nursing homes and hospitals were being assisted into buses and
ambulances and taken upstate. An estimated fifteen million
people—from Grand Isle, Louisiana, to Apalachicola, Florida—
were facing mandatory evacuations; all of the motels and
hotels and many of the shelters had already reached full capac-
ity as far north as Tennessee.

When Caroline heard that, she turned the television off.
She came to Point Clear to be nowhere else but Point Clear.
Anyway, her room was on the second floor, surely high enough
to be above floodwaters, and the structure itself was made of
brick. If that was good enough for Joseph and his wife, it should
be good enough for her. What she needed was supplies.

She went to grab her purse, then caught a glance of the clock radio and picked it up. Underneath, just like in hers at home, there was a compartment for batteries, in case you wanted to use the clock radio without the power cord; but there were no batteries in it.

She remembered seeing a convenience store somewhere between flowery Fairhope and Point Clear, so she set out walking along the grassy shoulder of the windy road until she found it, in a one-store town called Battles Wharf. The only flashlights they had left were miniature ones that hung on key rings, so she bought what they had, all five of them, in a variety of colors. And she stocked up on AA batteries, Slim Jims, beef jerky, little cans of Vienna Sausages, honey-roasted peanuts, cheese and crackers, Butterfingers, bags of chips and candy corn, and plenty of dollar bills and quarters for the Coke machines at the hotel.

On her way back to the Grand Hotel, she saw the weather turning from the south, a wall of rushing gray, and the wind felt good and cooled her. When she finally reached the hotel grounds, she thought only of getting to her room, freeing her arms of the bags, and flopping down on her king-size bed, but then she noticed the activity near one of the broadcast trucks, with lights and cameras, and as she came closer she saw that the person in front of the camera was CNN's Anderson Cooper. She'd been interested in him ever since she learned he was Gloria Vanderbilt's son, and she'd been interested in Gloria Vanderbilt ever since she heard her describe in an interview on television how she watched her son, Anderson Cooper's brother, jump from a Manhattan terrace to his death. Caroline saw the interview shortly after her father died, and though her father's death was an accident, he did die suddenly, and she knew her grief was Gloria Vanderbilt's grief, and she felt a connection to her, and to New York, and then to Anderson Cooper.

He looked smaller and more handsome than Caroline imagined he would look, like a small, tangible ad for success, with silver hair made messy by the wind as he spoke into his microphone about the potentials of storm surges.

Caroline watched until the camera and lights were shut off and Anderson Cooper went with some of the crew into the spa building. She looked up at the sky as she walked on. She was glad she'd thought to pack a raincoat.

6. | WHITE TENNIS SHOES

Caroline didn't exactly know how she would get away with staying behind at the hotel. She imagined she could simply hide under the bed. The hotel staff seemed to move about frantically, too busy, she hoped, to worry about hunting down guests who should have known anyway to leave if they were told to leave.

After a bath to revive her legs and feet from her tennis lesson and her long walk for supplies, she decided to venture out to the restaurant for dinner. She thought she might recognize someone from the news crews, maybe see Anderson Cooper again, but apparently nobody but Caroline wanted to dine in the restaurant with the panoramic view of the bay, now obscured by hurricane shutters. Throughout her meal of jambalaya pasta, all there was to listen to was the pleasing *shhhhhhh* of rain, then the occasional backdraft of wind blowing through the shutters.

After dinner, she wandered into the Birdcage bar, where Joseph would be spinning for Celtic Twilight Hour, but only the bartender was around, and he was packing away glasses and liquor bottles.

"We're open if you'd like a drink," he told her, "but it may take me a minute to find what you want."

She hated to bother him. "A Grey Goose and tonic, please," she said, because she hated not to have one last drink. She suddenly felt a surge of sentimentality about her life.

The bartender scanned through a couple of boxes before he located the Grey Goose and drew it up by its neck.

"How long do you think the hotel will be closed?" she asked.

He shook his head and reached for one of the few remaining glasses. "You never know. A few days, a week."

"Wow," she said.

"Oh yeah, unless we're blown completely away, we won't be closed for long."

She tried to smile but couldn't, and looked away. There was a grand piano. When the bartender was ready with her drink, she paid her bill, then walked over to the piano and touched the polished keys, though without pressing them. She wished she knew how to play.

Her drink was strong, so she drank only half of it, sipping it in different corners of the bar, as if she were trying it out, as if she were thinking about moving in. Then her eyes focused, and she realized she wasn't alone. Anderson Cooper was standing in the doorway.

For a moment he appeared relaxed, if not amused, but then his body seemed to stiffen and he looked caught, or recognized. It was an expression she'd seen from celebrities in New York, just before they looked away or darted off. But Anderson Cooper did neither. He was her first celebrity sighting to acknowledge her back with a smile.

"Saying goodbye to the bar?" he asked.

"I hope not," she said, "though it's not a good sign that *you're* here."

"No," he said and laughed, but laughed as though he'd heard that joke before.

Caroline smiled at him and was not sure what to say next. She liked his silver hair. It was thick like her father's. Her father was dead, and so was her grandfather, and that was why she was here. She thought if she said that, or said anything, he would understand.

"Please, be careful," he said.

She couldn't believe he was still talking to her, that at this moment she and Anderson Cooper were together. "I will," she said. "I'll be watching you."

"Thanks," he said, smiling, then vanished into the shadows of the lobby.

She stared blankly for a moment, then handed her glass to the bartender and walked out, feeling less alone and more confident about her decision. Soon this whole sprawling place, three buildings of room after room, would all be hers and Anderson Cooper's.

When she returned to her room, it was only nine o'clock. She was tired but not sleepy, but she thought she could convince herself to sleep if she was still long enough. Eventually, she did fall asleep, but she woke soon afterward. Her sleep the entire night was fitful, and she was happy to rise at daybreak. The *Today* show would be airing soon.

She was outside in the rain in her thin blue raincoat and hood when Al Roker appeared, smiling, carrying an umbrella. She watched the crew prep him on where to stand so that they could frame both the hotel and the bay behind him. They measured the light and watched the time while he muttered to himself, reciting, until they rolled, and then he confirmed what was believed yesterday, that Hurricane Ivan, a determined Category

Four, was on a direct course for Alabama's Gulf Coast and that the eye should pass over this beautiful little resort town of Point Clear early in the morning two days from now.

She hung around until the taping stopped and she was ready to get in out of the rain, which was picking up, beginning to slash, with whipping wind. She had five hours before checkout.

On her way back to her room, she passed a linen closet and on a whim tested the knob, and it turned. She looked around, then opened the door and grabbed a stack of towels. She couldn't believe it. She ran to her room, looked around once more, then shut the door. She made it! She'd have enough fresh towels for three or four days.

She hid the towels under the bed, along with her sacks of supplies from the convenience store. Then she called room service to order a feast of a breakfast, enough food to last her for the rest of the day, and while she waited for that to arrive, she packed up everything—her clothes, her laptop, her makeup and bath supplies—and stowed it all under the bed, too.

Room service still hadn't arrived, so she grabbed her purse and went down the hall to the Coke machine, and one by one she bought six bottles of water, all she could carry in one trip. She took them to her room and came back for more. When there were no waters left, she began buying bottles of Coke. Everything she needed to do had been done by the time her breakfast arrived, so she was able to relax and enjoy flipping back and forth to watch Al Roker and Anderson Cooper leaning into a wind too strong for umbrellas. They had to shout if they wanted to be heard, but half the time they were laughing, enjoying the immense strength of the weather. Behind them, the normally placid bay rocked with three-foot waves.

What she didn't eat, she hid under the bed and put the tray outside in the hallway.

"Ma'am," a voice said, startling her.

It was someone from housekeeping coming out of the room next door.

"You know you have to check out today, don't you?"

"Oh, yes," said Caroline. She looked at her watch. It was only ten o'clock. "I'll be out in another hour."

"By twelve at the latest."

"No problem. I will be," Caroline said and closed her door, but she stayed there by the door, pressing her ear to listen to the woman from housekeeping knock across the hall and call out, "Housekeeping." She heard the woman knock again and repeat herself, "Housekeeping," before opening the door. A minute or two later the door across the hall closed, and Caroline heard the woman moving to another door.

Caroline guessed it was time. She picked up the phone and called down to the front desk and told the man who answered she was checking out.

"Would you like for us to bill the charges to the credit card you used when checking in?"

"Yes, please," she said.

"And will you be needing the shuttle service, Ms. Berry?"

"Not this time. A friend is picking me up," she said. "So can I just leave my keys here in the room, or do I need to come down?"

"You can leave them in the room. That will be fine. You're all taken care of."

"Oh, good, thanks," she said.

"My pleasure. Have a safe trip, Ms. Berry."

"Thank you. You too," she said.

She hung up, and then it occurred to her to leave a tip for housekeeping, and she smiled, tucking a five-dollar bill under the edge of the desk lamp, a detail she was proud of. Then, after she used the bathroom once more, she crawled under the bed. What was the harm? If she got caught, she'd leave. She'd have no choice.

She was surprised there was plenty of room left under this king-size bed for more bags, more towels, more supplies. She didn't stick out at all. No one would think of looking for her here.

As time passed, she began to get nervous about what she was doing, thinking she'd made a terrible mistake, that somebody would find her, and what would she say? Her grandfather, if he were alive, would be humiliated.

She didn't hear any warning signs. Abruptly, there were three knocks on her door. "Housekeeping." Then three more, as if the woman were trying to break the door down. "Housekeeping," she repeated, almost shouting, it seemed to Caroline. Then the door opened, and Caroline held her breath. Footsteps approached, and then Caroline saw white tennis shoes come into view, moving toward the tip, then saw them stop, as if the woman was standing very still in order to hear if anyone was hiding in the room, as if she was waiting for an intake of breath. But Caroline held on, and the white tennis shoes continued to cross the room, and Caroline heard her slide the balcony door open and step out, as if she expected to find Caroline hiding there.

Caroline let her breath out easy. But the woman was coming back in, so Caroline quickly filled her lungs again and saw that the woman was bringing in one of the rockers. Caroline watched as the woman set the chair beside the bed, then went back out and brought in the other rocker, then the reddish, barrel-shaped table that had stood between them, which all the balconies were furnished with.

Caroline was feeling dizzy, but she didn't dare let out her breath. She held on until the woman had shut the balcony door, locked it, and traipsed her white tennis shoes past the bed and through the door to the hallway and the door had closed.

Caroline let out her breath in a gush and closed her eyes. She'd thought she might pass out. She'd never held her breath for so long. But it wasn't over yet. Surely someone would come by to make up the room. But maybe not. Maybe they would wait until after the hurricane. For now, bringing in what could become dangerous airborne debris would be enough. Safety first.

She played it safe herself, deciding to stay underneath the bed until one o'clock, though while staying underneath it, growing bored, hearing nothing from the hall since the woman entered the room, only the rhythmic wind and rain against the sliding-glass door, Caroline drifted off to sleep and didn't wake until almost two. She woke with a start, as if suddenly she realized she was asleep and it scared her.

She waited a moment, trying to calm herself, and when she was calm enough to hear beyond her breathing and still heard nothing in the hall, she slid out from under the bed and crept to the door. She listened as before—silence—so she opened it slightly and peeked out.

She flipped the latch to prop open her door, then gradually made it down the hall, and to another hall, and to another hall, and because there didn't appear to be an alarm system, and to make sure she wouldn't get locked out of her building or any building, she propped the doors open along the way with whatever was handy—a chair, a plant, a doormat. And then, when she reached the opposite end of the hotel, she peeked outside, toward the parking lot near the marina, where the broadcast trucks were parked. But they weren't there anymore. Anderson Cooper was gone. That could be good or bad, she didn't know.

What she knew was she was alone. The last one left. So why didn't she feel victorious? Now what?

7. | PAGES

After spending the last day and a half holed up in my room watching television and staring out at the bay and eating junk food, I guess I should be glad that the hurricane is almost here. But now the power is off, it's past midnight, now September 16, 2004, and it's pitch black. The light of my laptop will not last long. The hurricane should hit, the radio says, in two hours.

The National Weather Service is beginning to repeat itself, saying that Hurricane Ivan is still moving at 12 mph with maximum sustained winds at 135 mph, that it remains a Category Four, with hurricane force winds extending outward 105 miles from its center, and that its center isn't moving from my latitude and longitude.

So their advice, their primary advice, to me and anyone like me who should have evacuated is still the same: Stay away from windows.

The local broadcasters have interviewed people in Mobile who have evacuated for past hurricanes but this time have decided not to leave, and that makes me feel better, though tonight I've had vertigo, almost vomiting, and for a while I had to sit very still on the bed and not move my head, staring straight ahead in the dark and listening to the wind come in gusts. It's still coming in gusts, and I keep wondering if it will throw bricks or shingles through the glass, as I heard on the radio that it could. One person who called in was very concerned about political signs.

As I'm typing, I'm wondering if anyone will ever read these pages. If I died, would anyone read these pages?

To Emma: If something happens to me, you can just stay in my apartment and have my stuff, if you want it.

To Miriam: Although I didn't really like the work, you were very kind to me, especially on my last day.

To Casey: I'm sorry that I've never really paid attention to the hurricanes that hit Florida, though I don't know if one has actually hit where you are. I'm proud of you for being a wildlife biologist or botanist or whatever it is you do in the Everglades.

To Mom: I'm not sure you realized it, but in

our last phone call you hurt my feelings. It seems like you don't notice when I'm upset or you just choose to ignore it.

To Casey again: I'll never forget sitting in the big den chair, talking to some of Dad's friends after the funeral, and how you came in and stood in front of me and grabbed my shoulders and shook me, saying that I wasn't facing what had happened. I wasn't angry enough or crying enough and why was I just sitting there having a conversation with funeral guests, which is what I was supposed to be doing. It's what Mom was doing, too, but you didn't yell at her.

I wish I could write something to my father that he could see. I wish that he had written something to me. I don't even have one letter. I never went anywhere where he would have needed to write me a letter, and when he traveled for work, he would always just call. It has been nine years now since he died. When Casey and I see each other, which is not even once a year, we don't talk about him.

Casey doesn't go back to Tulsa any more than I do, but he went to Granddad's funeral. I hate that he was there and I wasn't. The last time I had a real conversation with Casey was the Christmas before last, when he went on about how our childhood was not as it appeared, not perfect, which is how he said I saw it. He didn't like how we all had to say dinner was good when it wasn't. And he hated the country club.

To Casey again: I hope you appreciate that I told you where the silver egg was at the Easter egg hunt at that place you hated.

Casey looks just like our father, not quite six feet, with brown hair, blue eyes, and sloping shoulders. Growing up, I used to envy their similarities, that on sight, people would know whose son he was.

After Dad was let go, his severance pay wasn't nearly as much as his old salary, and Mom wanted him to quit Southern Hills to save money. Dad and I didn't want to, so we stayed members. We had a lot of arguments with Mom about it. Casey and Mom didn't play tennis or golf.

But then Dad got the sports car, which seemed completely out of character. Before, he had driven an old Oldsmobile. And he was never flashy with anything else. He only had about five oxford work shirts and two suits. He wore a Timex watch. He got his hair cut for ten dollars at a barbershop where he'd always had it cut. Mom got her hair and nails done at Miss Jackson's and would get all her clothes either there or at Saks.

It's scary being alone here. I've moved the radio and my blankets and pillows to the bathtub, and the door is shut, and it's pitch black. The rain sounds like rocks hitting the glass, and it's thundering, and it's frightening hearing it in this confined space. Sometimes I hear a big, cartoonish whoosh, and *the whole hotel seems to shake. Part of me wants to go outside. I heard on the radio that you can step outside during the eye and it will be calm, could even be sunny if it's during the day, but you cannot stay out too long. I heard that during one hurricane the pressure was so great that all of the water was lifted out of the bay and that you could have walked to Mobile.*

8. | THE N / R AT UNION SQUARE

Moments before Ivan struck, the thin reception on the radio crackled into static, and then it was as if time had reversed itself and Caroline were transported back into the airplane that brought her here. Pressure built against her eardrums, and then, as if she'd gone deaf to the radio, to the flipping beat of her heart, all she could hear as she huddled in the bathtub, with her head sandwiched between pillows, was the massive blowing-roaring sound of the hurricane above her, ripping the roof from the hotel, she imagined, in one clean piece.

Some had said on the radio it would sound like a train, and it did, like the N/R subway when it first burst from the tunnel at Union Square, but perpetual, bursting and bursting, and she tried to do what her father would do whenever he flew any-where, which when she saw him do it embarrassed her, but here she was doing it now, holding her nose and blowing, and it worked. Her ears popped clear, but now it was as if Ivan were in the same room with her, about to sweep her away, to take her wherever the roof went. She felt terrified and wondered if her mother was even thinking about her. And then, finally, the wind and rain slowed, then stopped, and there was silence. She was in the eye.

She slowly removed the pillow over her head and turned on the key-ring flashlight she'd been squeezing in her hand. Its glow wasn't strong, but it was strong enough to illuminate a ceiling that was still there. She stepped out of the bathtub and eased the door open, very slowly, as if floodwater might rush in, or something else, an alligator or a shark the hurricane had dropped in her bedroom, she didn't know. But as she swept the frail beam across the floor and over the bed and walls, nothing looked changed.

She opened the curtains and then the balcony door. She could tell a little water had washed in through the frame and soaked the carpet. So far, that was the extent of the damage.

From the balcony rail, she swept her light in a circle, but it evaporated within a couple of feet and lit up nothing outside, though without it she could see that the trees were still and that the ground was pocked with something. The air was black and so was the bay, vaguely rocking in the distance, and then, making her jump, a zipper of waves crashed against the seawall. She raised her head slowly to see a clear, starry sky, a delicate crescent moon.

Although it was a sky she had seen before, she stared and stared and kept staring. She couldn't tear herself away. There was devastation all around her, yet she was protected from it. But for how much longer? The next hour? Next half hour? Next fifteen minutes? It really depended on where in the eye she was.

Then she lowered her head, because in her peripheral

vision she saw something ghostly sailing past, something in the water, she thought at first, but it was too elegant as it floated by to be actually floating, and then she recognized the beak and the ruffled feather-tips of its outspread wings. A pelican venturing out, like she was.

Caroline had lived through dozens of tornadoes back in Oklahoma. If she was at school when the warning siren sounded, she'd file out of class with all the other students and sit down in the hallway with her hands laced over her head. If she was at home, it was much more fun. Before heading down to the basement with candles and a portable radio where they'd eat snacks and play cards on blankets, the whole family would go outside to feel the air get cooler and watch the sky get darker, sometimes even seeing a twister twist in the distance with the frightening movement of a snake. Before they had the house with the basement, they had to go to her mom's walk-in closet or a bathroom, or when the tornado was predicted to be especially bad, they went to her grandfather's storm cellar, a dark, damp place with rock walls.

During the worst tornadoes, her family was a close family, sometimes huddled together, candlelight between them. That had been important to Caroline, but this seemed just as important, even though she was alone. She wanted to remember this always. She focused her eyes, and far to the horizon, across the bay, a rim of the eye wall crept into view, wiping away stars, sparking and glowing soundlessly with lightning.

She closed the door in a hurry, locked it, then drew the curtains closed and ran back to the bathroom and waited, with pillows in place, for the wind and rain to return. For the N/R to burst through the tunnel.

PART THREE

9.| THE SWIMMER

The eye wall had passed three hours ago. By all preliminary accounts, most of the damage had been done east of where Caroline was, in Gulf Shores and Orange Beach and along the Florida panhandle. Caroline listened to the radio and was told that everyone should still stay inside, that power lines were down and conditions were ripe for flash floods, lightning, and tornadoes. She opened the curtains, and in the bluish light before daybreak, she saw the fishing pier was destroyed. Much of the railing that lined the sidewalk was still standing, but the bricks from the sidewalk were broken up and some were scattered over the lawn. The water looked deeper and choppy. She felt it was safe to go outside. She put on her raincoat, but it was not raining.

Her tennis shoes sank into the saturated grass, then into the muddy beach, but when she glanced back at the hotel, there didn't appear to be any real damage. There were downed branches on the orange roof, and a door leaned against a palm tree. It was a door that didn't match any of the doors she'd seen at the hotel—more like the front door to someone's house, with glass inserts completely intact, but apparently ripped off its hinges and now leaning neatly out of the way.

She walked down the beach toward the bay houses, where there were more wrecked piers, one after the other, and a floating overturned boat. In the distance, she saw a man. He was tall and thin and was standing ankle-deep in the water. As she moved closer, she wondered if he was trying to salvage a boat she couldn't see, but then she saw he was stretching his arms behind his back and was wearing a swimsuit.

She kept walking toward him. The past two days she had been sneaking around, trying so hard to be hidden, and it surprised her now that she was walking toward him. When she got closer, she stood a moment and looked at his long back, which broadened at the shoulders, then she noticed his elbows, curved inward—nearly touching—as he stretched. His arms looked like an hourglass. He was double-jointed.

She was standing ten feet behind him now. "Excuse me," she said.

He turned around. His dark short hair came to a V on his forehead. He had very dark, intense eyes, but then he smiled. "Doesn't the water look beautiful?"

"It looks murky," she said, "but I suppose there's beauty in that. Are you going to swim in it?"

"Sure," he said. "Today's a good day for that."

She watched the bay tilt and surge with waves. She felt exhausted but giddy from lack of sleep and having made it through. "I've been staying at the hotel," she said. "I was supposed to evacuate, but I stayed anyway. You're the only one who knows."

"So you made it," he said. He looked up and down the

beach, as if to confirm that they were the only two who had stayed and made it.

"I made it," she said, and she suddenly felt emotional and hoped she would not cry. "My name's Caroline." She held out her hand.

His hand enclosed hers. "My name is Walker."

She saw flecks of gray in his black hair. He was tall, six foot six maybe. "Do you live around here?" she said.

He pulled away his hand and motioned behind him. "Well, my parents do, just a few houses down. And for right now, anyway, I live in their guesthouse."

"You didn't evacuate either?"

"No, I toughed it out. My parents were already out of town, so I just told them I'd leave, that I'd just get in the car and drive north."

"My mom doesn't know either," Caroline said. "I guess she thinks I've gone."

"So we're both not supposed to be here," he said. He looked at her as if he already knew her.

She smiled at him. She thought, *He seems like me.* Her grandfather used to say that she had a lot going on behind her eyes. Walker had a lot going on behind his eyes. Afraid she'd been silently staring at him too long, she finally spoke. "I think I'm going to go back in and fall asleep."

"That's good," he said. "I'm going to do that soon myself."

"Okay," she said and turned away, then turned back toward him. "It was nice to meet you, Walker."

He lowered his head and leaned to the side until he was seeing her at eye level. "Maybe we'll meet each other again, Caroline," he said.

"I'd like to," she said. She felt all her defenses were down, and she was needing a friend. He was someone she would want to be friends with. She thought about asking him to meet her that night, but instead she said, "Please, be careful."

He didn't turn around. He began to walk into the water. "I've swum in this bay a million times," he said, and then when he was deep enough, he lay back in the water and began to backstroke, his long arms moving slowly and deliberately.

10. | CIRCLING THE PROPERTY

When Caroline returned to her room, she cleared the pillows and blankets out of the bathtub and lay down on the bed in a melting collapse. She wondered, briefly, if this was the result of survival—this purity of self, this calm, this sleep that was enveloping her. She felt she was changing. Into what, she didn't know. But she knew she would be stronger.

When she woke several hours later, she woke thirsty and reached under the bed for a water. Outside, seagulls clamored in a tangle of cries. She took a long drink, then another, then reached for the clock radio on the nightstand, forgetting that it was still sitting on the floor in the bathroom where she'd left it. She thought she should rise, should stay informed, should slide the door open to let in fresh air. But the seagulls were a little loud. She twisted the cap back on the bottle, then fell asleep again.

When she woke the second time, she woke revived, alert,

fast, was up on her feet before realizing she wanted up. She stepped around the rockers and peeked through the curtains, and in the late afternoon sun she saw a group of men patrolling the grounds, some with hard hats, some without, all wearing boots, appearing to inspect the damage. They didn't look like hotel employees who might check her room—anyway, there were over four hundred rooms, and she was in one of the older ones. Probably they would check the newer ones first, and she guessed that it would be housekeeping doing the checking, and she could explain her way out of it if she had to. She wasn't going to worry about that until it happened. The important thing was she was still alive, after all, and she went into the bathroom and tested the water, and it ran, so she filled the bathtub. The water was room temperature, but she was fine with that and turned the clock radio on, keeping the volume low, before getting in.

The worst news was that the death toll had risen to twelve, with seven people dying in Florida that day in tornadoes spun off from the hurricane. There was other news. For her area, free ice, food, and water were available at the Daphne Civic Center. A 7 P.M. to 7 A.M. curfew was in effect. The rusting of grass and trees observed in and around Fairhope was a result of salt saturation. And the power had been shut off deliberately before the hurricane, as a precautionary measure, and should be back on tomorrow. That was the best news.

After her bath, she turned the radio off and dressed in the last light of twilight. It was after seven o'clock, but she waited until complete darkness before parting the curtains all the way and sliding open her door and moving a rocking chair out onto the balcony. Then she carried out the barrel table, then her dinner, and she ate in the peace of night, to the high water of the bay lapping against the seawall, to the glancing silver of the sky on the water, to fish leaping—all around her, it seemed—with the gentlest kiss of sound.

In a strange, wildly unpredictable way, this had been what she'd hoped to find on this trip. This contentment, this peace. She would someday write a novel. She believed she would. About what, she didn't know exactly, but she believed she could, and that was all that mattered.

On occasion, when the nearby oak tree creaked, or just when she felt a presence and looked down toward the bay houses, she thought of that interesting Walker fellow, thinking that he might be passing by, or someone might. But each time she found herself alone, and that was okay. It was nice to share moments like this with someone. But it was nice to have moments like this at all, ever.

The peace disappeared the following morning, when Caroline woke to the sound of chain saws chewing up fallen branches along the hotel grounds and beyond. Whenever one halted, there were others in the distance. Through the glass of the door, she watched men collecting the sidewalk bricks and boards from piers and fencing into piles. Only workmen, though. No one in a hotel uniform.

She slipped outside without anyone seeing her, then skipped across the lawn, wide of the hotel, as if she might live down where the bay houses were, walking with her head up, as if she shouldn't be anywhere else. Ahead of her someone stood at the back of a pickup truck lowering the tailgate. The truck was filled with rolls of yellow CAUTION tape and orange netting.

The man glanced at her, and she smiled.

"Excuse me," she said, and he raised his eyebrows. "Would you happen to know when the hotel will be opening back up?"

"Not for a few more days. The target date's the twentieth."

"Oh, okay," she said.

"We have to make sure it's safe, so watch yourself," he said.

"I will," she said, and waved and walked on. She passed other workmen, and they said nothing to her. Some noticed her. Some didn't. Some nodded, so she nodded.

After circling the property and inspecting the damage herself, she was amazed by how little of it there was. She didn't see any broken windows, and not one of the ancient live oaks had been uprooted or knocked down, not even the ones by the duck pond with limbs that twisted along the ground like snakes, then rose in direct vertical lines like separate trees. The ducks swam unruffled where they always swam. When it was clear, she ran to the entrance that she'd left propped open with a flashlight, then went back to her room.

She was trying to decide what to eat this time, a Slim Jim with a Butterfinger or cheese and crackers and candy corn, when the power kicked on with a vibrating hum—the lamps, the television, Anderson Cooper, the air-conditioning—and then shut off again.

She sat on the edge of her bed with hands clasped between her knees. *Come on, come on*, she begged.

Again the power surged. She waited with trepidation for it to shut off, but it didn't. And then it still didn't. It was on for good, it seemed, and she was thrilled. In a couple of hours, there would be ice down the hall, and she could drink a cold Coke for a change.

She propped her pillows against the headboard, then settled back with candy corn and a Slim Jim, a new combo, and began watching Anderson Cooper, who now seemed like someone she knew because she knew he was more handsome in reality than on TV. He was broadcasting from Gulf Shores. It looked worse where he was, with flooding and a collapsed business behind him. He was saying something about someone called Chucky, who weighed one thousand pounds and was twelve feet long. She started to listen more carefully and understood then that Chucky was an alligator that had escaped from a nearby zoo, and authorities were currently searching for him.

Caroline felt joyous, almost crying for the fact that she and Anderson Cooper and that swimmer she met, Walker, and the ducks and live oaks and even Chucky had survived something as dangerous as Hurricane Ivan.

And then her emotion shifted to shame as CNN began airing the latest footage of the damage, sweeping aerial shots of hundreds and hundreds of beachfront homes and shops and condos, whether massive or not, buried or half-buried under sand or water. Some, and at times all in a row, were flattened piles of yellow lumber. Some had been lofted into the air and spun around, and some were roofless, some split wide open.

The coverage continued all along the Alabama coast, in Gulf Shores and Orange Beach, and as the helicopter continued, so did the destruction, all along the Florida coast, in Perdido Key, Pensacola Beach, Navarre Beach, Okaloosa Island, Destin, Panama City Beach, St. Joseph Peninsula. It was like a war zone, or worse. Worse than where Caroline was, and she had been right in the center. Her flippancy in the face of this—or was it obstinacy? or hubris? whatever it was about herself that had convinced her to remain—horrified her. And from that moment on, she couldn't wait to check back into the hotel so she could be legitimate again.

Her life became a chore to fill up the time with dignity until the twentieth, when the hotel would hopefully reopen. Today was the seventeenth. Tomorrow, Saturday, would be the eighteenth. She was reminded of her life in New York, counting down days to the weekend, waiting, doing nothing, hoping for something. She was more determined than ever not to return to that life. Not in New York and, if she could help it, not here.

During the day she kept a low profile by spending most of her time in her room, watching television, reading, listening to music on her laptop (mostly the Waterboys CD that Joseph had given her), and eating unhealthily, though routinely she left to spy out the small windows of exit doors, on the lookout for housekeeping.

But during the night, late at night, she found new interests. There was only one security guard posted at the entrance of the hotel, but he was not hard to elude, and there seemed to be no one wandering around the actual hotel. On the night of the seventeenth, she ventured to the Birdcage bar and practiced for hours on the grand piano, until she'd taught herself three songs: "Chopsticks," "Mary Had a Little Lamb," and "Jingle Bells." And on the night of the eighteenth, she ventured outside to the pool area. The pools were still cluttered with deck furniture and debris, but she managed to clean up one of the hot tubs and even locate the switches to turn on the jets and hot water. So she relaxed under the stars and moon and ate her only remaining food. She was glad it was her last.

Tomorrow morning she would trek back to the Battles Wharf Mini-Mart for more food, though different food this time. And hopefully, hopefully, hopefully tomorrow, the nineteenth, would really be her last day on the lam. She wanted to check back in more than anything. To have soap, clean linen, room service, tennis lessons, and not to be anonymous—that was a life.

11. | THE SUNDAY PAPER

The next day at the Battles Wharf Mini-Mart, she bought two small cans of ravioli with pop tops she could fit into her purse for later, and for now a fountain Coke and a pepperoni Hot Pocket that she heated in their microwave. She decided to eat outside on the curb because she didn't want to chance a conversation with the friendly gray-haired woman at the register. She just wasn't in the mood. She had gotten comfortable with being alone.

She truly enjoyed eating something hot, and as she was finishing, she happened to glance behind her at the *Mobile Register* in the yellow newspaper bin. It was the Sunday paper, and there was a full-color picture of flooded streets in downtown Mobile, with its antebellum homes and giant magnolias. Then she noticed in the bottom right corner a small column with the headline *Former swimming star reported missing*. The picture was of Walker.

She stood up, then sat down again and searched in her

purse for change but didn't have any, so she stood up, threw her cup, paper plate, and napkin into the trash can, then went back inside with two dollars out and asked if the woman at the register could break them to get a paper.

"You know," the woman said, not moving to take Caroline's money or to open the drawer, "those papers just came in. The first we've seen since Ivan. We're lucky to have them. Some won't yet other places."

Caroline nodded and laid the bills on the counter, then pushed them almost into the woman's hand, thinking this would hurry her, and perhaps it did. The woman opened the drawer, then counted out the quarters. "Did you make out okay in the hurricane?" she asked.

"I did." Caroline felt she had to say something. "Did you?"

"We did all right," the woman said. "My husband lost his toolshed, and we have a lot of downed trees, but we can't complain." She smiled and handed Caroline the quarters.

"That's good, thanks," Caroline said and was outside before the woman had a chance to say another word. She put five quarters into the box, then pulled the latch and grabbed a paper, reading as she walked around the corner, out of sight.

> *Former swimming star Walker Galloway, a Stanford University graduate and NCAA champion in the 200-yard backstroke, has been reported missing. The thirty-year-old resident of Point Clear disappeared sometime in the last week.*
>
> *Galloway's father, Tom Galloway, reported his son missing at 7 P.M. Saturday, five days after he was last seen. An investigation is being conducted by the Fairhope Police Department.*

Caroline didn't have to think about what to do. She went to the pay phone and dialed the operator, then asked to be connected to the Fairhope police.

She told the woman on the phone that she had seen the missing man, Walker Galloway, three days ago, and the dispatcher told her that she would need to come in.

"I don't have a car," Caroline said. "I'm from New York visiting."

"You picked a fine time to visit. I'll send someone to come and get you. Where are you?"

"The Battles Wharf Mini-Mart."

"Fifteen minutes," the woman said.

While she waited for the police, Caroline tore the article out of the paper and studied the picture of Walker. He was younger here and had longer hair. He was in a pool. His head was tilted. This was the same way he had looked at her.

She did not know if what she had to say would help at all. She thought of her father's accident and didn't believe Walker would be found alive. When her father died, the truck driver who had killed him came to the police station to tell his side of the story to her mother and Casey. Caroline had just started college and was living in the dorm, and they went down there without her. Her mother and Casey explained to Caroline that it was clearly not the truck driver's fault. There were other drivers on the road to attest to that, but the truck driver was the last person to see her father before he died. It was midafternoon following a rain shower, with the sun piercing the clouds, glinting off the pavement, making it—she always imagined—like the surface of a river. And perhaps at the most blinding moment for her father, heading into a curve, he slid or swerved, and had he slid or swerved right, where the ground was open between staggered trees, he probably would have survived. But he went left, and the truck driver had a clear view, looking down from his cab into her father's low convertible. He was the witness to her father's death.

Caroline hoped she was not the witness to Walker's death. She hoped that he hadn't drowned. How could a champion swimmer have drowned? *I've swum in this bay a million times.* Maybe he had decided to leave after his swim, to drive north as he'd told his parents he would do. Maybe he was off in some hotel room in northern Alabama or Tennessee or even Georgia and not calling his parents as Caroline was not calling her mother. Was her mother frantic now? Caroline should have already called her.

At this moment, Caroline believed Walker was alive.

A black police car with a blue lightning stripe appeared and pulled into the small gravel lane between the store and the gas pumps. Caroline waved and walked over to the passenger side as quickly as she could. She didn't really understand why, but she hoped the woman at the register didn't see her. This was her first time in a police car, and she felt nervous, as if she were finally being caught for all that she had done wrong.

The officer half-circled around into the road, then introduced himself in a friendly manner. He was almost pretty. He looked like he did not have to shave. His brown hair was carefully swept to the side. She wondered if he'd become a police officer in part to compensate for his face.

She asked him if Point Clear had a police station, and he explained that it didn't. Most of Point Clear, including the area around the Grand Hotel, was in Fairhope's jurisdiction.

"I drove through Fairhope on the way in," Caroline said. "There are lots of flowers."

"Yeah, it's quite a production," he said. "The city has its own horticulturalist, used to be the mayor, and every month or so, they change them all out with different ones."

She smiled and tried to think of something else to say, but couldn't. Dismayed, she looked above her, where this road had been canopied before, and now split trees and branches and Spanish moss lay in tremendous heaps on each side of the road, sometimes in the road. All the vegetation looked washed out, not green but gray-green, or at times a bright rust, and she remembered what she'd heard on the radio, how the seawater from the gulf had stricken certain areas with sudden death. There was no pattern, though, just as with the houses. One house would be pristine with absolutely no damage, and at the next a tree would have fallen through the roof.

The Fairhope police station was on the edge of the small downtown and didn't look like a police station, but more like a welcome center made of new red bricks. Caroline asked if there was a jail in back, and he said there was.

When she walked inside, the police officer shook her hand and turned her over to the female dispatcher up front, who said she was the one Caroline had talked to on the phone.

"Detective Bowers will be out in just a minute," she said. She sat behind thick protective glass, which Caroline guessed was bulletproof.

Caroline peered in through the glass and noticed about sixteen video screens, which showed all parts of the police station and the jail. "This is sure a state-of-the-art police station," Caroline said.

"It's much better than the last one," the woman said. She was thin with long orange-brown hair, and her shoulders slumped. "Over there, I always had to put buckets out when it rained. All over the place." Then she held out her hands as if she were holding a bucket, then moved them again, pretending to hold another bucket. "Take a look around," she said.

Caroline saw a glass case across the room with an exhibit of old police memorabilia, but decided to walk over to something framed on the wall that looked like an old document. Written in cursive handwriting that was hard to see was a criminal docket dated July 1909. Caroline focused and read one of the complaints. *Using obscene language in the presence of ladies. Complaint by Ira Powell.* It did not say whom the complaint was against.

"Excuse me." Detective Bowers was dressed in plain clothes and wore a holster and gun. He looked gruff, like a detective should. He shifted the clipboard in his hands and introduced himself.

"Hi," she said and shook his hand. "I'm Caroline Berry."

"We can talk in here." He motioned to his right, then punched a code into a door that led to a small office. There were two chairs and a small table, and Caroline sat closest to the door. There was a window that faced the street, and an empty coat rack was in the corner.

"So, tell me when you last saw Walker Galloway."

Caroline took a breath. She had already rehearsed in her mind how she would begin. "It was the morning after the hurricane, and I was walking on the beach toward the bay houses on the south side of the Grand Hotel to see if there was any damage. I saw him standing just inside the water's edge. I remember it sort of surprised me because he was wearing a bathing suit. I'd never met him before. I'm on vacation from New York. Anyway, we talked about the hurricane, that we were glad to have made it through, and he told me he was going swimming, then he said he was going back to his house and go to sleep, like I said I was going to do."

She waited a moment while the detective took notes.

"Did he say anything about anywhere else he might be going?" the detective said.

"He told me that he was supposed to drive north and just stay at some hotel. I think he said that about the hotel. Maybe that he was just driving north. That's what he told his parents, so they wouldn't worry, I guess."

"Did he say anything unusual at all?"

Caroline shook her head. "No, he seemed in good spirits, like I was, just happy that the hurricane was over and everything was all right. Then he started to swim out into the bay. The backstroke."

The detective finished up his writing, then said, "Well, his father is confident that he will show up. Walker may have gone somewhere with somebody and is just not thinking about calling. He's done that before. It's just because of the hurricane that his parents are more worried. Especially his mother."

"I understand that," she said. "I still need to call my mother."

"Anything else?" he said.

"No," she said.

The detective stood up, then Caroline stood up.

He folded back a blank page on his clipboard and asked her to write down her name and number. Caroline felt nervous, and hoped she wouldn't stumble. "I'm staying at a friend's house now, and I don't know his number."

"Who?" the detective said.

"The tennis pro at the Grand Hotel," Caroline said. "His name is Joseph. I don't even know his last name. I don't know anyone, but I play tennis, and he and his wife are letting me stay with them until the hotel reopens, which is tomorrow. I'll be checked in at the Grand Hotel tomorrow."

"Just write that down here," he said.

Caroline wrote, *Caroline Berry. Staying at the Grand Hotel.*

"You need a ride back to the tennis pro's?"

"No, no," she said. "I'd like to look around at the town."

"Not much is open," he said.

"That's okay," Caroline said, and was hurrying to get out of there. She began to sweat, and knew the dizziness was not far away.

"Thank you for coming in," he said.

"Sure," Caroline said, heading for the door. When she walked through the lobby, she passed a woman who looked a bit like her mother, wearing a beige linen top and matching pants. Her highlighted blond hair was poufed up. "Can you give me directions to Sea Cliff Drive?" she asked the dispatcher.

Caroline could not help but smile. She felt that this was a sign that everything would be all right, that Walker was not really missing at all, not in a community like this, where flowers were potted on trash cans and the police station served as a welcome center. She started to walk toward the traffic light, in the direction of downtown. She would go find a pay phone and call her mother, and then a cab.

12. | CALLING FROM A SHELTER NORTH OF BIRMINGHAM

Most of the shops in Fairhope were still boarded up, with an occasional message to Ivan spray painted on them, telling him to go away, though one was more generous, saying hello. A few store owners were in the process of removing large sheets of plywood from their windows, using drills to undo the screws. On the corner of what appeared to be the main intersection stood an old-timey sidewalk clock that reminded Caroline of the one in New York in front of the Flatiron Building. This would be a nice place to live, she thought. Here or in one of the bay houses in Point Clear. She looked around for a pay phone but didn't see one anywhere.

Finally, she found one outside a grocery store that was still boarded up, though only across the front, not where the doors were, on the side, and spray painted on the plywood were the words OPEN, WATER, ICE, and HOT MEALS.

Not until she had the phone in her hand and began to dial the numbers of her phone card did she decide to call Emma first. She'd thought about calling Emma before, from the hotel, but didn't want to risk having it traced back to her.

The phone only rang once before Emma answered.

"Hey," Caroline said.

"Caroline, thank God," Emma said, then shushed someone. In the background, Caroline heard someone she thought was Anthony saying, "Quiet on the set."

"Your mother and I have been worried sick," said Emma.

"Really?"

"We've gone back and forth on the phone, and we've been trying to reach you at the Grand Hotel. Miriam called here and left a sweet message. Can you believe that? Rita didn't call, of course. To be honest, I'm relieved. I would've been afraid to talk to her."

"I've been at a shelter," Caroline said. "It's awful. I've been sleeping in a high school gym in a donated sleeping bag. Kids were screaming."

"That sounds terrible. Are you still there?"

"Yeah, I'm still here—well, outside on a pay phone. Did I come up on Caller ID?"

"No, out of area."

"Well, okay," Caroline said. "I should be able to check back into the hotel tomorrow. You can call me there sometime."

"Would you like me to call your mom for you?"

"No, no," said Caroline. "I'm about to call her now. I was just curious if you'd heard from her, if she was worried. So I'm about to call her now. I better go. Good luck with your film."

"You could hear that?" Emma asked. "I have to say I'm loving it as the director. I love bossing Anthony around. And every-thing's fine with the building. The super came out when we were shooting an exterior, but it's fine now."

Caroline normally would have worried about something like this, but now it seemed trivial. "All right, then, Emma. I'll talk to you soon."

"Bye, Caroline. I'm glad you're okay. I didn't even know about the hurricane until your mother called, but after that, I was glued to CNN."

"Me too," Caroline said, and realized immediately, that she had slipped. "I couldn't believe they had cable at the shelter."

"This whole time I kept wishing that you had a cell phone. You really do need to get one. I swear you're the only person in the tristate area who doesn't have one. Even my grandmother has one."

"Maybe I'll get one when I get back. I better go, okay. I'll talk to you soon."

"All right, bye," Emma said in a sweet, high voice.

"Bye," Caroline said, her voice breaking. She hung up the phone, then immediately lifted the receiver and put in her phone card number again, then her mother's number.

"Mom," she said, when her mother answered, "I'm all right. I'm at a shelter."

"Oh, Caroline, thank goodness. I've been so worried. I called the hotel and couldn't get an answer. Then I called your apartment and talked to Emma. I really do love Emma."

"That's nice, Mom," Caroline said, "but I can't believe you were worried. You didn't seem worried before."

"Well, I didn't really know what was going to happen before. Then it was all over the news, and all my bridge friends were asking about you, and I guess that is what really worried me because they were so worried. Now, where are you?"

Caroline watched a man across the street drag an enormous brown awning down an alley, with the mangled aluminum poles scraping the pavement. "I'm at a shelter just north of Birmingham, and it's terrible, and I don't want to talk about it. I'll be back at the hotel tomorrow," she said. "I told you the hurricane was coming."

"I know, but it just didn't seem real then. I never think about hurricanes."

"Well, I didn't either, but you know Casey lives in Florida."

"I know," her mother said. "I feel terrible, really I do, Caroline, so if you don't mind, I'd like to come down there and see you, then go on and see Casey. Next week, if that's okay."

"Are you serious?"

"Yes, the end of next week. Just for a night, because David wants to go to Saint Augustine to see the Fountain of Youth, then on to Charleston, South Carolina, to tour historic homes."

"Well, that's a hell of a trip."

"So, I'll see you on Thursday, just for one night."

Caroline shook her head. "Okay," she said.

"Let's hang up now," her mother said.

Caroline hated it when her mother cut off conversations like that—"Let's hang up now."

"I love you," her mother said.

"I love you, too," Caroline said, but she did not feel good saying it. She hung up the phone and walked into the grocery store, depressed and defeated.

Though the smell of fried chicken cheered her up a bit. She got two breasts, mashed potatoes, and green beans, all hot, in a Styrofoam box. She opened a cold can of Coke, poured it into a cup of ice, and had a drink, then peeled off a bite of chicken and ate that, all before she paid at the register. Then she asked the cashier how to get a cab.

"Call Eastern Shore Taxi," the cashier said.

Caroline went back to the phone outside and asked the operator to connect her.

A woman answered the phone with a punchy, direct voice, and Caroline asked if she could be picked up at Greer's Food Tiger. The woman on the other line said, "Be there in just a minute."

Caroline ate her meal while she waited. She thought it was nice to eat with a fork for a change, even if it was plastic. She was halfway finished when a town car pulled up. She'd save the leftovers for dinner. They seemed like they would be better than the ravioli.

A woman with short brown hair rolled down her window. "You call for a ride?"

"I did," Caroline said, then got into the back. "Grand Hotel," she said, then, thinking better of it, "a house on the far side of the Grand Hotel, actually."

"You got it," the woman said.

Because of her large size, Caroline guessed, the woman didn't wear a seat belt. She drove in a confident way, with only one hand on the wheel.

"You from out of town?" she said.

"I am," Caroline said. "From New York."

"Uh-huh," she said. "I'm good with faces, and I ain't— *haven't*, not ain't—seen yours around here. How'd you like that hurricane?" she said and smiled.

"I'm glad it's over," Caroline said.

"Sure wish it would have uprooted every one of those Bush and Kerry signs. I'm sick of seeing them. I guess it looks like Bush will win again."

The woman was driving through a residential section of Fairhope Caroline hadn't seen before, which was a virtual thicket of trees and downed power lines. She seemed to know in advance which streets were clear and which weren't.

"How'd *you* like the hurricane?" asked Caroline.

The woman laughed and took her one hand from the wheel to adjust the air-conditioning from its highest setting to the next one lower. "I survived." Then Caroline saw round brown eyes looking at her in the rearview mirror. "I've almost been killed lots of times, though not in a hurricane. I've been in a wreck, flew right through the window and cracked my head open, and I still don't wear a seat belt. They're just not comfortable to me. And when I was a baby, I was scalded in bathwater because my brother filled up my bath with only hot water and didn't realize what he'd done. I don't hold it against him, though. How could I? And I've almost died other times, too. We don't have time enough in this ride for me to tell you all the ways."

Caroline nodded, giving a sympathetic look. They were stopped in a line of cars leading up to the hotel. Trucks with mounted grapples were clearing branches and other debris from the road. A policeman was directing traffic.

"See that cop," the woman said, then took her hand off the wheel and pointed. "He's a cop cop. If you're speeding, just a little bit, he'll give you a ticket, and he's never too friendly. You know what I mean? He's what I call a cop cop. Now if he were just a cop, he'd be something different. If you see a cop on the side of the road giving someone a ticket, and you're friendly with that cop and you wave at him, he'll wave back. A cop cop won't do that. Do you know what I mean?"

"I think I do," Caroline said.

As they approached the entrance to the hotel, the woman slowed. "Now, where was that house?"

"The first one coming up, over here on the right," said

Caroline. "And you don't have to go all the way down the drive. You can just let me out at the road."

The woman nodded. "You got it," she said, pulling in, then once she stopped, Caroline noticed there was no meter. The woman shifted into park. "Ten dollars," she said.

Caroline gave her thirteen and thanked her.

"You bet," the woman said. "I'll know your face next time."

Caroline shut the door, waved, and began walking up the long wooded drive, dodging clumps of Spanish moss the size of clothes baskets, and when the woman had backed out and driven away, Caroline cut through the trees and side yard, skirting the house as much as possible, until she'd reached the sand-covered sidewalk and then the beach itself, where she had met Walker. Where she had seen him stretching his arms. Where he had shaken her hand. *Maybe we'll meet each other again, Caroline.* She could see him walking into the water, much rougher than it was now, then lying back and beginning to backstroke with unexpected grace. She looked out into the bay where he'd gone and watched the surface carve images between whitecaps. She stood for a long time, searching, she supposed, but knowing it was illogical, believing that any moment he would appear and she would be the first one to see him return.

13. | HOUSEKEEPING

Caroline was surprised to find she could get back into her building and her room. From how her day had gone—the news about Walker, the police, the phone call with her mother—she expected homelessness, another obstacle. It was odd that housekeeping hadn't appeared if the hotel was reopening tomorrow.

She took a long shower that was hot enough to make the walls bead with water, and then she put on pajamas and took her billfold and the ice bucket down the hall. When she returned, she poured a Coke, then lay back on the bed and turned on her laptop. She thought she might understand her day better if she worked it out of her. Maybe she'd remember something, or realize what she actually thought.

The knocking at her door didn't startle her at first. It was too unexpected. Only after she'd heard it, a series of three raps on her door, did she process the sound and flinch, not knowing what to do, where to hide, if she should hide.

"Housekeeping," she expected to hear.

"Police, Detective Bowers," she expected to hear.

But whoever it was didn't speak. Caroline simply heard three more raps on the door.

"Caroline," she heard. A man's voice. An undemanding voice. One she couldn't place.

She felt she had no choice. She rose from the bed but moved hesitantly toward the door. "Coming," she said, and then it occurred to her who it must be, saying "Walker?" as she opened the door, but seeing someone else.

"Daniel?" she said. He was in a red shirt this time, still Nike, thin and long-sleeved. She saw his lean muscles beneath the shirt.

"I'm sorry to surprise you," he said. "I found out from Joseph where you were."

"Oh," Caroline said, not quite understanding how Joseph could know.

Daniel stood in the hall and told her that Walker was a childhood friend, his best friend, and that Walker's father, after speaking to the police, had told him that a young woman who was staying at the Grand Hotel tennis pro's house saw Walker on the beach the morning after the hurricane. "Of course, you're not staying there. You're here. Joseph figured out that you must be here. He had your room number from your lesson."

Her hair was wet and she didn't have on any makeup, but she was not going to let that matter. "Please, come inside." She held her arm out, and then, as if seeing the room anew, she suddenly felt embarrassed by how she'd been living.

The two rocking chairs and plastic barrel were wedged between the foot of the bed and the armoire that held the television. The trash can overflowed with empty twenty-ounce Coke bottles and water bottles. Slim Jim, Butterfinger, beef jerky, and many other wrappers were all over the place—on the bed, on the bedside table—along with more Coke and water bottles that wouldn't fit into the trash can. Her recently opened Coke was sitting delicately on a book on the bed next to her laptop, and next to that was her Styrofoam container with fried chicken.

"What in the world is going on here?" he said, laughing, stepping over a week's worth of dirty clothes and dirty towels that were seeping out from the closet.

"I wanted to stay," Caroline said. "I didn't want to go to a shelter."

"You know, you really could have stayed at Joseph's house. All you had to do was ask. He's very generous, you know."

She thought about Joseph reading her his story. It was an intimate thing for him to have done. "It never occurred to me," she said, then shook her head. "But I wouldn't have wanted to impose. I had only met him that one time, for that one lesson."

"Well, all right. He doesn't care. Nobody cares."

Caroline looked away.

"I don't mean that. I mean, I care. Of course, I'm glad you made it through. I wanted to see you again anyway."

"You did?" Caroline said.

His eyes began to water, becoming even greener, but his voice was steady. "Can I ask you some questions about Walker?"

"Sure," she said. She pointed at the rocking chairs. "We can sit here, if that's okay."

He moved everything to a clear space—the chairs, the barrel between them, and they sat down. "Did he seem depressed when you talked to him?"

"No," she said. "Just the opposite. He seemed happy."

"Like manically happy?" Daniel said. "Walker could have serious mood swings. At Stanford, after his coach yelled at him, Walker disappeared for a week."

"No," said Caroline, "he seemed content. He seemed happy and content."

"And he was swimming backstroke?"

"Yes."

"How far did he swim out into the water?"

"I only saw him go about four or five strokes. I didn't want to watch him too long."

He gripped the arms of his chair. "Why is that?"

"Because I felt like I'd been staring at him too long anyway. I didn't want him to stop swimming and see me looking at him. I was afraid he'd think I was looking at him because he was double-jointed. Or because he was swimming at all. And I felt so out of it, having stayed up all night in the hurricane, that I just wanted to get into bed and fall asleep."

"And he told you he was going to go fall asleep, too?"

"Yes," she said, nodding. "I said I was going back inside to go to sleep, and he told me he was going to do that soon himself. 'Good,' I remember he said, like he was concerned about me, like he could see how tired I was, then he told me he was going to go to sleep soon himself."

"At home?"

"I assumed so," she said.

He took a deep breath. "Can you tell me anything else?"

Caroline didn't know what she could say that she hadn't told Detective Bowers, except for how she'd felt. "I felt like we made some kind of connection there," she said. "Not like an attraction, but something else, like we were the same person, if that makes any sense."

Daniel smiled. He looked around. "Walker drank Cokes and ate candy around the clock. It drove his coaches crazy. In college, he got obsessed with computer games, just like when he was first obsessed with swimming, and his dorm room looked just like your hotel room."

"Really?" Caroline said.

Daniel leaned forward and rested his arms on his knees. "What kind of bathing suit did he have on? Do you remember?"

"Speedo, I think," she said, but didn't quite know why it mattered, unless, she realized, to identify his body, and she was surprised Detective Bowers hadn't asked the question himself. She thought for a moment. "I'm pretty sure it even had the word Speedo on it," she said. "His swimsuit was blue, like a sapphire blue."

He was quiet for a moment, and Caroline tried to picture Walker as she first saw him. "It was short," she said, "but it had square legs. And there were white stripes on the side."

"That's good," he said. He nodded. "You've been really helpful, Caroline, but I need to get back to Walker's parents. They're feeling frantic right now. His car was there. His computer was there. Nothing unusual. No suitcase was gone. His wallet was there. His keys were there, but the guesthouse was unlocked, like he intended to come back. But I know he often left the door unlocked, so that may not mean anything."

"So," said Caroline, "do you think he drowned?"

Daniel shook his head, then lowered his head in his hands. His fingers were long. She imagined if she held his hand, it would feel like Walker's.

"There's so much debris in the bay," he said. "Trees, telephone poles, sections of decking from piers, ladders, sailboat masts. There could be nets, ropes, and traps from shrimpers, oystermen, crabbers. There could be anything. That's what Walker's parents are afraid of. He was used to swimming in the bay. He was swimming to the Mobile side when he was like twelve. But he could have hit his head or gotten tangled up in something. You know, the bay is closed for a reason."

She touched his arm loosely, then her fingers fell, and he sat back in his chair.

"He was the most naturally gifted swimmer," Daniel said. "Everyone always said that. He could swim every stroke better than almost anyone in the world. Backstroke was his best, though. He made the cut for the Olympic trials when he was fourteen. That's unheard of. It was like whatever he decided to do, he just did."

He nodded, and Caroline didn't know what to say, and then he stood up. "I should probably go. It's getting late," he said. He hesitated. "Do you want to come stay with me at my parents' house?"

"Oh, no, I'm fine here, but thanks," Caroline said, thinking that she had almost made it and didn't want to quit now.

"You sure?" he said.

"Yeah, I can check back in tomorrow."

"All right," he said, and Caroline followed him toward the door, watching him look around once more at her mess. And then he stopped by the closet, reached in, and pulled out two laundry bags that were clipped on a hanger.

"I'm going to take some of this trash out for you," he said.

"Really?" she said. "I didn't know where to take it. The hotel must have locked away every trash can." Though, now that she thought about it, she had never actually tried to find any trash cans. She only recalled not having seen any around.

"That's all right," he said, shaking one of the bags open. "I don't mind." He pushed his sleeves up, and Caroline watched him fill one bag until it bulged and he had to tie the drawstring in a knot for it to stay closed. Then she watched him do the same with the other.

"I guess I should've helped," she said, as he was finishing.

"No," he said. "No problem."

She opened the door for him, hoping she wasn't making a mistake not going with him, and when he was out in the hall, she watched him walk away, a bag in each hand. Here was a world-class tennis player carrying away her trash. It was an extraordinarily nice thing for him to do, yet she wondered why she couldn't have done it for herself.

14. | A NEW ROOM

Caroline woke early, with the image in her mind of her father's sports car crushed against the grille of a tractor-trailer. It was something she had seen only in a photo, the one for the article in *Tulsa World* about the accident, about his dying at the scene. But it was something she would never forget, how her father's new red Alfa Romeo Spider had looked like nothing more than a crumpled bumper hanging off an old truck.

It was the morning of the twentieth, so Caroline didn't try to go back to sleep but rose to pack. With no signs of house-keeping yet, she turned on the television, keeping the volume low, and listened as Al Roker explained that a rare phenomenon appeared to be developing with Ivan, now an extratropical low in the Atlantic. After arcing eastward through the South, it was now circling back, gathering strength, assembling itself into a tropical depression, and heading toward the peninsula of Florida, just north of the Everglades, where Casey was, and could actually cross through the Gulf of Mexico and return to the Gulf Coast in a few days. Not to Alabama this time, but to Louisiana or Texas.

When she finished her packing, which mostly amounted to dirty clothes by now, she eased her door open and peeked out. There was a cart of supplies sitting in front of a room at the far end of the hall, so she grabbed her bags and rushed for the exit in the opposite direction.

She followed the covered walkway to the lobby entrance, saying hello to the valet drivers. She felt something akin to nostalgia, seeing the orange-yellow tiles of the lobby floor again, the exposed brick and pinewood walls, and as she looked past the steps that led to an octagonal tavernlike sitting room, with a double-sided fireplace and beams of lumber crisscrossing the ceiling, and to the Birdcage bar beyond it, she remembered the night she sat at the piano and taught herself to play. So much had happened to her lately, she almost believed she was checking in after a long sabbatical.

Since she had saved money on lodging the last five days, she asked at the front desk if she could have one of their best rooms. The man in the gray jacket and black tie asked if one on the fourth floor in the spa building, facing the marina, would suit her, and she said yes it would. She looked forward to a change of scenery.

She handed him her credit card. "So the whole hotel is up and running again already?" she asked.

"Almost," he said. "We prepped the newest buildings first, and the one you will be staying in is our newest."

"Oh, that sounds perfect," she said, excited not only about her new room but also in learning she'd been right about their paying attention to the new buildings first.

And when she opened the door, she thought the room was perfect—brighter, cleaner, much newer than her last room, and with higher ceilings. She drew back the curtains, revealing French doors instead of sliding glass. The marina was still virtually empty of boats, and she thought of what Daniel had told her last night about the bay being closed. The only traffic now was a flock of pelicans calmly riding the waves.

Since she'd run out of soap a couple of days ago and had been bathing with shampoo, she took a shower before doing anything else, then called room service to have a lunch brought up—something healthy this time, a salad—then laundry service to have her dirty clothes picked up. As she bagged them and set them outside her door, she thought of Daniel carrying out her trash. She felt happy doing what she was supposed to do, being where she was supposed to be.

After lunch, she put on the outfit she hadn't worn since her first day because of the heat. It was almost cool today. She was going to see Joseph. She felt she owed him an explanation.

In front of Court One, there were four women sitting around a wrought-iron table with a green umbrella. They were tennis women, dressed in skirts and matching tops and visors. They looked exactly like the women who played doubles at Southern Hills when she was growing up. She imagined they wore sunglasses when they played and hit angle volleys.

She walked to the far court, which faced the road that Walker must have lived on, and maybe Daniel. Joseph looked as if he was at the end of a lesson. He and a girl who appeared to be about Caroline's age were picking up balls with green metal hoppers. He waved Caroline over when he saw her.

"Jaysus, Caroline," Joseph said. "What's the story?"

She shook her head. "I'm sorry if I put you in a bad position."

"Nah," he said. "So, how was it? Was it like the time at the U.S. Open when I couldn't get into my bleeding room that

Daniel had gotten me and I had to sleep at Grand Central and security kept moving me to different parts of the station?"

"A little," she said, laughing. "But security never caught me."

"Of course not," he said.

Caroline folded her arms. "Well, I'm legitimate now. I just checked in. I have a room in the spa building that faces the marina."

Joseph raised his eyebrows. "That's really nice for you."

She nodded, then leaned in. "Do you know him? Walker?"

"Yeah, yeah," Joseph said. "He's a big music fan, like me. We've had some conversations. I think we have to stay positive."

The girl came up carrying a hopper full of balls. Joseph took it from her and lifted it above the shopping cart, turning it upside down, and the balls tumbled in. "Ready for serves?" he said.

"Not really," the girl said.

"I'm sorry to interrupt," Caroline said.

"Ah, she needs the break," Joseph said, nodding toward the girl. "This is Chandler. She's from New York, too, but lives here now."

Caroline smiled. "Really, where'd you live?"

"Gramercy Park," Chandler said, swaying with her racquet limp in her hand. Her blue overgrip was loose at the base and was beginning to unravel. She wore shorts and a T-shirt. She could have been thirty or a little older, but she had the demeanor of a teenager.

"It's beautiful there," Caroline said. "I live at Union Square, on Fifteenth Street."

"Really?" Chandler said. "I love Union Square."

For a moment, Caroline felt nostalgic, and it seemed to her that Chandler did, too, and Caroline wondered if Chandler was picturing skateboarders, the dog run, the farmer's market on the weekend, the spirals of smoke from tables of incense. It seemed like a world away.

"And here you both are in Point Clear," Joseph said. "You two should play sometime. Chandler played in juniors, too."

"Where?" Caroline asked.

"In Arkansas," Chandler said. "How about you?"

"Right next door. Oklahoma. I'm from Tulsa."

"Oh, really?" Chandler said. "I'm from Fort Smith, and to us, Tulsa was really the big time."

Caroline laughed. "That's funny. I've never thought of it that way."

Joseph nodded. "All right, we better get started again."

"We'll have to play sometime," Chandler said, with a slight wave of her hand, then turned away, walking to the baseline.

"I'd love to take another lesson," Caroline said to Joseph.

"That'd be grand," Joseph said. "Come by later, and we'll find a time."

"Okay," Caroline said. "Also, could I use your phone inside? I need to call a cab to go into town."

"Oh, no, no way, you can't do that," he said, and he pointed away in a sword-thrusting motion. "You just take me car, the orange Volvo with the fairy stickers," he said and laughed. "It's not like a new Volvo or anything, but it's just sitting over there in the parking lot, and the keys are always in it."

"Well, if you don't mind," she said.

"Mind?" he said, waving an arm and walking off. "If I'm here, you can use it. I've got insurance. Nothing to worry about."

"Well, okay," she said. "Thanks a lot." She was excited to drive again. It would be her first time in years.

She liked Joseph's Volvo. Apart from the stickers of Irish

fairies, women with wings and torn dresses and wavy red hair, it reminded her of her father's cars, before he bought the sports car. She liked that the door creaked and was difficult to close, and that the driver's seat looked as if it had been partially eaten by dogs, and that the windows, even though electric, took longer to drop than if you had to roll them down yourself. She knew the road in front of the hotel led to Fairhope, and she knew the public library in Fairhope was next door to the police station, but she didn't remember how to get from one to the other. Surely, that couldn't be too difficult.

The difficult part would come at the library, where she hoped to learn more about Walker. There would be newspaper articles there and high-speed Internet. Maybe, if she knew more about him, she'd remember a detail she was forgetting or didn't realize she'd noticed. Maybe that could help solve the mystery of where he was. Not likely, she understood, but she wanted to know more about who he was, regardless. This person who had made her feel more important just for having met him.

15.| THE INFORMATION

It took Caroline only a moment on the online catalog to find hundreds of articles on Walker Galloway from the *Mobile Register* and *Fairhope Courier*.

She asked the librarian for help and was led to a back room and given a stack of reels of microfilm she didn't know what to do with. Research had been something she avoided in college. So after the librarian loaded the first reel and showed her how to go forward and backward, slowly or fast, how to rotate, how to zoom, how to focus, Caroline leaned closer to the screen and began sifting through the information.

Mostly she saw listings of stats from swim meets, which read more like stock-market quotes than results she was used to seeing from tennis tournaments; they gave Walker's event, name, age, team, seed time, finals time, and points. But from these, she could see what Daniel had said—he could swim any stroke, but backstroke was his best. Later, in college at Stanford, he swam the backstroke and the individual medley, which was equal distances of all four strokes: butterfly, backstroke, breast-stroke, and freestyle. There was no monumental find in these stats, but they fascinated Caroline nonetheless. Then she found four feature articles on Walker that seemed to chart his entire career.

The first feature declared him a "swimming phenom." The article began, "Walker Galloway not only swims fast for his age, he swims fast for anyone's age. He's very strong and very flexible." There was a picture of him, a young teenager, with his goggles pushed up on his forehead, eating from a bag of chips. Walker was quoted as saying, "I'll have no problem qualifying for U.S. Nationals," and the article confirmed that he didn't. Walker could swim before he could walk. He could hold his breath for four and a half minutes. A coach was quoted as saying, "He is the kind of swimmer I have spent my career dreaming of."

The second feature was about his receiving a swimming scholarship to Stanford. There was a yearbook picture of him wearing a jacket and tie. He said that he chose Stanford not only because of the school's rich history in swimming, especially backstroke, but because it was in a sunny part of the country. He had been considering Auburn but thought Stanford would be better for him. He needed the weather to be sunny year-round, like it was in Point Clear, and he liked living near the water. He was shy, the article said, but a very likable young man with a sly sense of humor. His classmates from Bayside Academy were always trying to make him laugh. He was a perfectionist and had a compulsion to do better at every race. "His performances continue to be remarkable," his high school coach said, "but Galloway is not happy with them."

The third feature had a picture of him in a pool with bright blue water, finishing a race, glancing with no emotion up at the scoreboard. He had taken third in the 200-meter backstroke at the 1992 Olympic trials. The article was about his devastation. If you took third at the trials, you would not be a part of the Olympic team. Apparently, coming in third at the Olympic trials was more heartbreaking than coming in fourth at the actual Olympics. Galloway wanted to quit swimming altogether, the article said.

The last feature had a picture of Walker swimming. It was taken from above, and the black lane line at the bottom of the pool looked jagged in the water. Walker's arms looked thin, thinner than when Caroline met him. The article explained that he was double-jointed in his elbows, knees, and ankles, a swimmer's gift, the hyperextension providing extra inches of reach and range of movement. Caroline was happy to learn that Walker had not quit swimming and had won an NCAA championship for Stanford in his senior year. But she was as dismayed as Walker must have been when he swam the 200-yard backstroke a second slower than his goal time and just missed setting the American record. It would be Galloway's last race, the article said. He already had a job lined up after graduation as a computer programmer.

Caroline hoped that Walker was happier after his retirement from swimming, that he didn't feel like a failure. She hoped that he was an excellent programmer and loved his work. And if he wanted to, which she guessed he would, he could disappear into the maze of cubicles that she imagined they had in computer programming jobs. Maybe Walker preferred that no one knew who he was, what he had almost accomplished. She imagined he didn't want to hear, "Ah, you almost made it to the Olympics. You were so close."

Caroline left the microfilm room not certain what to think. She got on one of the computers to check her e-mail. She didn't have any, of course, only junk mail. Caroline hardly ever sent e-mails to friends. She wondered what Walker preferred—e-mailing his friends or calling. He seemed so contradictory. Even though he must have been interested in technology and gadgets, she bet he preferred to call. It seemed so much easier to call.

She then decided she would Google Daniel, but realized that she didn't know his last name. She typed in "Daniel tennis Point Clear" and discovered that his name was Daniel Lanaux. So she typed in "Daniel Lanaux" and got four thousand sixty results.

A lot of what she found reminded her of what she found for Walker, just his name listed with scores and with other players' names. But there were also interviews. Like Walker, he had gone to Stanford, and in his senior year, he was their #1 player. He, too, won an NCAA championship. He'd been on the ATP tour for eight years, and two of those years he had to sit out because of a shoulder injury. (Caroline couldn't help but laugh, imagining Joseph saying, "The Seagull hurt his wing.") When Daniel returned to the sport after his injury, his game had even improved. Daniel said his best assets were his serve and his determination. He was quoted as saying, "I've always been ranked between 150 and 200, but my goals are much higher." Daniel, she read, worked with a "nutritionist, spiritual adviser, acupuncturist, yoga instructor, and digital photographer who analyzed his strokes." And, Caroline thought, with a mad Irishman.

An article in *USA Today* about Daniel was titled "The Outskirts of Greatness." In that article, which appeared several months ago, was a quote from Nick Bollettieri, who said, "Let me tell you this: Lanaux is thirty. If he is going to be a top-tier player, he would have to defy all law, and I don't see God intervening." Caroline had known a few players in juniors who had gone to Bollettieri's camp in Florida, but Caroline had been afraid to go. She had heard there was a lot of running, and that wasn't her favorite thing. She didn't think Bollettieri knew everything, anyway. His "Nick's Picks" at the U.S. Open were almost always wrong.

With the article in *USA Today* was a picture of Daniel at the 2003 U.S. Open. It was taken on a changeover, and he was sitting in a chair under an umbrella, drinking a bottle of Evian. He was on a side court without many spectators. Caroline had gone to the Open that year, and on the first two days had wandered all over the grounds. She could have seen him there.

The best news Caroline saw about Daniel was from an interview dated just a few weeks ago. "I don't have a house. I don't have a wife or kids. I don't have a girlfriend. I kind of feel like a prizefighter who comes to this secret place of Point Clear and hides out and trains and then I go out into the world and see how good I can be."

16. | SPOTLIGHTS IN LIVE OAKS

After returning Joseph's car, Caroline set up a lesson for the next morning. She told him she loved the Waterboys CD he'd loaned her and would make sure to bring it back to him tomorrow, then she walked the easy walk back to her new room in the spa building. Her clothes had been cleaned and bagged and were waiting for her just inside her door. She looked down at her fingernails, then decided she wanted a manicure and pedicure. She called the spa, but there were no available times then or for the rest of the day. "Sorry, we're busier than normal," the receptionist told Caroline. "Ivan."

Caroline asked about the next day and got an appointment to follow her tennis lesson, though when she was told the price, she almost changed her mind. But she had gotten used to having her nails done every week in New York, where it was a cheap luxury, and she was overdue. Anyway, it wouldn't be so bad to stay put, to begin to relax right now in this newer, roomier room, and she called room service to place an order for dinner, salad again. She was a new person.

She opened the bag of clean clothes, pulled out a pair of pajamas, then went to open her curtains for the view when the phone rang. She expected it to be room service saying they were out of something, but she hoped it was her mother calling to say she wasn't coming to Point Clear next week after all— she'd bailed out before. But it was neither of them. It was Daniel, and when she heard nervousness in his voice, she knew what the news would be, that Walker's body had been found, that he was dead. But Daniel didn't have that news or any news. He was only calling, he said, to see if she would like to have dinner with him tomorrow night.

"I hate to think of your being cooped up in that hotel eating every meal by yourself," he said. "I know how awful that can be after a while."

"Well, sure, I'd love to go," she said. "Thank you."

"My pleasure," he said, and then laughed, and Caroline knew why he was laughing. That's what everyone who answered the phone at the Grand Hotel said if you thanked them for something.

Daniel asked if she liked Thai food, and she said there was a place in New York, Bangkok Café, that she ordered delivery from at least once a week. He said they'd go to Fairhope, to Renaissance Café, where every Tuesday was Thai night because the owner, who was the chef, had lived in Thailand. He'd pick her up at seven.

The next day she did everything she could to prepare for her first date in four months, which seemed a long time to go when you were twenty-seven. Her mother had commented that Caroline needed to be going out, having all kinds of passionate, sexual affairs with all kinds of men. Those were her mother's words, and Caroline supposed there was some wisdom in them.

After her breakup with the medical student, she didn't date for a few months, and then there was her last date, four months ago, a terrible blind date set up by a tennis friend of hers. During dinner, her date talked on and on about how bored he was all the time with everyone, and Caroline asked him if he was bored then, and he said, "No more bored than I am with anyone else." After that she hadn't wanted to date anyone else.

But Daniel was different, or she was different, so she felt confident about seeing him. She knew what she would wear— a black skirt and a lilac V-neck. She would wear her silver necklace with the little diamond, and her small silver earrings with the small lilac stones. She would wear slingback black heels, though in New York if she walked in them too long her feet hurt. The first time she wore them, in the summer, one heel got caught in a subway grate, and she fell out of her shoe.

She laid out her outfit on the bed, planning to iron later, then changed into pants and a spaghetti-strap sweater, feeling kind of sexy already, and took the elevator to the first floor to the spa. She checked in at the front desk, and a tall, broad Swedish-looking fellow, or maybe he was of Finnish descent, like Emma was, walked her to the salon.

The pedicure came first, and her treatment was much fancier than at the nail place in New York. Her feet were dipped in paraffin wax, which felt weird but didn't hurt, and afterward they were smooth. The manicure was next, and her hands were dipped in wax also, but they didn't feel as transformed as her feet did. She asked to have her nails painted with clear polish, and the woman doing them looked disappointed. Caroline had always been a fan of clean, simple nails. She thought of Rita and how she exercised barefoot and her toes were always painted red.

One of the hairstylists was sitting in a chair reading a magazine, so Caroline asked if she could just have a couple of highlights.

"Ya don't really need them," the stylist said. She was young, pretty, and blond, and Caroline thought she detected an Irish accent.

"Are you from Ireland?" she asked, thinking of Joseph, wondering if she knew him.

"No, Wales," she said, then untied her smock to reveal a T-shirt that said, YOU CAN TAKE THE GIRL OUT OF WALES, BUT NOT THE WALES OUT OF THE GIRL. "Me mum just sent me this T-shirt in a care package. She's been worried about me because of the hurricane."

"That's nice," Caroline said, amazed by the worldly people she had met in Alabama. She looked at herself in the mirror, then glanced back at the Welsh girl. "You don't think I need a few highlights in the front? I have my first date in four months tonight."

The girl smiled and stepped closer, examining Caroline's hair. "Well, of course, then. I know how ya feel. It's psychological. Ya have to look your best. I met my husband when I was doing hair on a cruise ship. Then I had spiky black hair with purple streaks. He fell in love with me right away."

So she got her highlights and got a story of how a Welsh girl fell in love with an Alabama boy and settled down in Point Clear. Caroline always enjoyed listening to people talk about their lives. She would ask questions about everything and leave feeling she knew the person, when the person would not know her at all.

In her room, after showering and ironing her outfit, with seven fast approaching, Caroline applied her makeup and could not stop smiling. It was hard for her to believe that she was going out with Daniel, that he would want to go out with her. She thought that if this was to be her only date with him that it would be all right, that she could think back on it years from now and know that she went out with one of the best tennis players in the world, the best college player in his day at Stanford. The whole scenario seemed so dreamy, and then she thought of Walker, but she did not want to think about him tonight. She dried her hair, slightly curled her ends, then put on a matching lacy bra and underwear and dressed. While she waited for Daniel, she practiced how she should sit, looking at the mirror that was opposite the bed.

Daniel knocked three times. Caroline smiled, then answered the door. There he was, standing before her, in olive pants, a crisp white shirt, and with the smell of aftershave. "You look beautiful," he said.

"Really?" she said. "Thank you. You look very nice yourself, different from, you know, your tennis clothes. People always do."

"You look different, too," he said, "a very nice different."

"Okay," she said, beginning to feel awkward, "I'm looking forward to Thai night."

"And tomorrow," he said, "we have Celtic Twilight Hour."

"Really?" she said, excited that he already wanted to see her tomorrow, then remembering. "Joseph said Fridays, though."

"Nope. He's been demoted to Wednesdays. They think that because it's a slow night anyway, because it's church night, that he can bring in some business."

"Well, I'm definitely there," Caroline said.

"Oh, good," Daniel said, and his hand touched her back a moment as they walked down the hall.

They took the elevator to the indoor parking lot, and

Daniel led her to a black Volkswagen Jetta and opened the door for her.

As he backed out, he smiled and said, "I hear you drove Joseph's car."

"I did," she said. "It was so fun. I haven't driven in forever."

Daniel drove through the exit gate and took a left at the main road, the same way Caroline had driven into town.

"You know, before coming here," Caroline said, "I hadn't even left the island of Manhattan for two years, except for one time when I went to Tulsa for Christmas."

"You're from Tulsa?" Daniel asked.

"Yeah," Caroline said.

"I've been there a few times," Daniel said.

So far, this was not the best conversation. Caroline looked out the window. It was very dark outside, and the road seemed more winding than it did in the day. Stars were scattered across the sky, and there was a half-moon.

"I travel all the time," he said. "Even now, I'm supposed to be in China."

Caroline knew why he didn't go, and she felt better knowing that he, too, was trying not to think of Walker and failing.

"How'd you do in Delray Beach?" she asked.

"The quarters," he said. "Radio Dublin tell you I was there?"

She laughed. "He did." Then she tried to act cool, and not too much like a fan. But a fan was what she felt like after looking up all his results and interviews on the Internet.

Daniel was able to find a parking spot on the street not far from the restaurant. Caroline noticed that the boards had been taken off nearly all the store windows. She saw a store called Uptown, which looked as if it sold women's clothes, and a bookstore called Page & Palette.

"That's a good bookstore," Daniel said. "And there's

another one, too, Over the Transom, with new and used books," he said and pointed. "A few blocks that way."

Caroline nodded and thought Joseph might have told him something about her being a writer.

The Renaissance Café was on the second floor of a white stucco building. They walked up steep outside stairs, and Caroline took the steps carefully because of her heels. On the balcony, where there were tables and chairs but where no one was sitting, she stopped a moment and looked out onto Fairhope's small downtown.

There was a black awning above the door, which he held open for her. Once inside, in the dim lighting, she saw a mirrored bar, and the walls were yellow and trimmed in white. All the tables were small and square, and each had a white tablecloth, a candle in a crystal candleholder, and a slender vase with a single yellow flower that Caroline thought was a mum.

They were led to a table in the back. He pulled a chair out for her, which she was not expecting, so she almost sat in another one. The place was not crowded but not empty either. She noticed a man moving from one table to another and guessed he must be the owner.

Their waitress began to explain what Thai food was, and Daniel gave Caroline a look, but they politely listened to the explanation about the different spices.

Daniel ordered a spicy shrimp dish, and Caroline ordered green curry chicken. Daniel asked if she'd like wine or a drink. Caroline decided to have a Grey Goose and tonic, and Daniel said he'd have the same, which was a relief to Caroline. She felt they both needed something strong right away.

"I don't normally drink," Daniel said. He laughed. "What I normally have, when it isn't water or protein powder in water, is something like wheatgrass juice. Do you drink?"

"Not really," Caroline said and smiled. "I used to," she said, "a lot in college."

"I did as a freshman in college, right at first, then I realized why I was there and really focused on my tennis."

Caroline thought of her short career in college tennis. She never even played a match. The Golden Hurricane. That was Tulsa's mascot. It had never made much sense to her.

The waitress brought their drinks, then colorful Asian-noodle-and-vegetable salads, then a warm roll for each of them, which seemed odd, but which Caroline was happy about. Daniel began with his salad and Caroline started with the drink, then pinched off a bite of her roll.

They ate and talked more about college. Daniel had been a computer science major. Like Walker must have been, Caroline thought. She told him she had majored in English, with a minor in philosophy. She always liked to add that. Then she told him about her lack of a career and her hope to write a novel.

"My advice," Daniel said, "is just to write, and to tell yourself you can make a living at it. That's what I did with tennis. People used to always ask me, 'How long are you planning to play?' That was when I was like twenty-three, which seemed crazy, because I knew I was going to make a living out of tennis and stay on the tour for a long time. Now I'm thirty and I'm playing my best tennis."

Caroline nodded. She didn't want to speak. She wanted to listen.

"There are some guys on the tour who start out thinking, 'I'll play a year or two. I'd like to see Asia.' They're traveling around playing and using their father's credit cards. Those are the guys to stay away from."

The owner of the restaurant came by and sat in the empty chair next to Daniel. "You're the tennis player, right?"

"Right," Daniel said. "Good memory. And this is Caroline."

The owner tipped his head. "Nice to meet you. Is everything all right?"

"It's delicious," Caroline said, and Daniel agreed.

"Good, good," the man said, and got up and walked into the kitchen.

Daniel leaned closer to Caroline. "That's amazing," he said. "I've only been here once or twice before. I wish I had that kind of memory."

"Me too," Caroline said, though she was thinking that Daniel was easily memorable and probably something of a local celebrity. "I'm observant, and I can always remember names of authors, actors, or directors, but not always the names of people that I just meet."

After they finished their meal, they ordered another round of drinks.

"So do you have agents or sponsors?" she asked.

"Well, I get free racquets and clothes. And I've had help here and there from people, but mostly I do everything on my own. I've found that I like doing things on my own."

She smiled. "For a while growing up, I got free racquets from Prince, and I remember getting a few T-shirts."

Daniel nodded, swirling his glass a moment before taking a drink. "Joseph said you're good, by the way—that you could have played college. Why'd you quit?"

Caroline pulled on a strand of hair and let go. "I did play, for a few weeks my freshman year, but my father died, and I just stopped playing. Maybe I would've stopped playing anyway, I don't know."

"I'm sorry," he said. "How did he die?"

"Car accident," she said.

"I'm sorry," he said.

"It's been nine years," she said, picking up her glass, then, realizing it was empty, she set it back down. "I'm all right with it."

The candle was flickering between them, and he put his hand over it for a moment, then drew it back. "I hate to admit this after two drinks, but I'm feeling a little drunk," he said.

She put her hand over the candle. It cast an eerie light as she moved her hand back and forth. "Want to play tennis?" she said. "I'd like to see if I can return one of your serves."

He laughed and looked down at what he was wearing. "Like this?"

"Well, I could just put on tennis shoes. But you'd have to stay the same."

"All right," he said. "But I could hurt you."

"No, you won't," she said. She figured, if she had to, she could just get out of the way.

After he paid the bill, he drove her back to the hotel, and he waited in the car while she ran upstairs and changed her shoes. She figured she could use one of his racquets.

They drove over to the courts, even though it was a short drive. She felt elated being there with him. He opened the trunk, got out two racquets, and found three good balls. "All right," he said, "but I'm a little nervous about this."

"Oh, I can take it. My best assets are my return of serve and my determination."

He turned to her with a half-smile, as if the claim was familiar, then he went behind the shed where Joseph kept his cart of balls and the tractorlike machine that swept the courts. The lights flashed on, growing bright in a few seconds. She walked to the forehand side of the far side of the court and readied herself to return a 130 mph serve.

Daniel stretched and swung a few practice swings, then he served very softly to her.

"Oh, come on," Caroline said, hitting it back.

He served a bit faster, and she hit it back again. "That's good," he said.

Then he served a full motion out wide, and she did not come anywhere close to hitting it.

"That's more like it," she said. "But this time, serve it right at me."

He served, and a second too late yelled, "Watch out."

She turned and the ball hit her shoulder.

He ran to the net. "Oh, I'm sorry. I shouldn't have done that."

"No, no. I told you to." There was a mark on her arm.

He touched her skin, softly, and she flinched.

"Oh, I hate that I did that," he said. Then he held her a moment and leaned down and kissed her. She was surprised, and her body seemed to collapse within his. She liked how he kissed, his tongue moving slowly into her mouth. When she pulled away and saw his eyes, she felt a kind of shock all over that seemed to stay. She felt she could go anywhere with him.

"How is it feeling?" He pointed to her arm.

"Fine," she said. "I'm fine."

She asked if he would walk her to her room.

"Sure," he said. He gathered the balls, and the two racquets fell into his hands so naturally. She loved his hands. He went to turn off the lights. She was already walking, and he jogged to reach her. He was beautiful moving through the darkness in his white shirt. She wasn't going to worry about anything. She would live in the present and enjoy it. They walked across the street, onto the path to the spa building, spotlights in the live oaks leading their way.

Inside the elevator the light was bright, and she looked away from him. Neither said a word. They walked down the hall to her room. "I could come in," he said.

"Oh, I don't know," she said.

"Okay," he said. "But Celtic Twilight Hour tomorrow. It starts at seven, and I can pick you up then, and we'll walk over together."

"Sure," she said. And then she remembered something she'd been meaning to ask him. "Where do you live?"

He smiled. "My parents live here in Point Clear about a mile away, but I don't always live with them. I also have an apartment in Atlanta that I share with two other players. And I have another coach there."

"Oh, I was just wondering."

"I'm always traveling," he said.

"Oh, I know," she said.

He leaned in to kiss her again, and she kissed him back. This time she kissed him longer in a determined way, and when they stopped, he looked at her and raised an eyebrow.

"I'll see you tomorrow," she said, turning around and quickly slipping in her key card, then closing the door behind her. She didn't want things with him to be over and awkward in the morning.

And thinking about him, enveloped by joy, she seemed to glide across the room and out onto the balcony. She held on to the railing. The marina was calm. She watched and listened to one small boat, with its sail tied down, rock in the water. There was a coolness on her ankles and her arms. She touched the tender spot on her arm. It was a marvelous night.

17. | A PRETTY FOOT

The next morning Caroline met Joseph on the court for another lesson. He said hello, then began a lecture on how the pros play the margins. "Visualize where you want to hit the ball," he said. He walked three feet in from the baseline and singles sideline, and then made an X in the clay with his shoe. Then he moved three feet in from the center mark and made another X, then another one three feet in from the other singles sideline. "This is where you want to hit the ball. The biggest misconception in tennis is that the pros aim for the lines. They don't. Not unless it's a serve. There it's like throwing darts. Otherwise it's too risky. When they hit the line, it's like they're missing."

After hitting at the Xs for an hour, Caroline felt elated from exercise and wanted more, deciding to run on the treadmill in the spa, and the running was actually pleasant as she looked out onto the sunlit bay. She thought about what Joseph had taught her, how it applied to life. You should visualize where you want to go, and if you take risks, they should be calculated.

When she got back to her room, she showered, then took a nap. That evening, when she dressed for her date, wearing black pants and a beige top with a scoop neck and cap sleeves, she felt revived and thin.

Daniel wore jeans this time, and a pale blue Oxford with the sleeves rolled up. She was getting used to seeing him in regular clothes.

Celtic Twilight Hour had a decent crowd already, and there were two other Irish guys there with Joseph, along with his wife, who was quiet and pretty, and his daughter, a blond, wispy eight-year-old. Caroline recognized her. She'd seen her jumping rope barefoot, going full speed around the perimeter of a tennis court.

"This is Caroline," he said to his daughter. "She's a tennis player, like you."

Caroline smiled. She liked being called a tennis player.

She and Daniel sat off from the others and the music so they could talk. They didn't talk much, though. Daniel drank Guinness, and justified this because it was Celtic Twilight Hour and he had to support the Celt. Caroline had Amstel Light.

Joseph was something to see, on a little stage in the corner of the room, spinning music that had a bluegrass sound, with banjos, mandolins, fiddles, and stringed instruments she didn't recognize. And with yearning, sometimes drunken Irish voices.

Joseph danced slightly. Sometimes he introduced a song, or recited a line of poetry, or dedicated a song to his wife or his daughter, who went home early, since the place was getting busier and rowdier. Hotel guests hearing the music came in, and Joseph welcomed them. "Here ye, here ye, step right on in. Let's trip da light fandango and go like ninety."

Around eleven, Caroline and Daniel went back to her room. They'd had more to drink than the night before, and now when she opened the door, he followed her in. She didn't turn on the lights. The balcony curtains were open, and a reddish light came from the harbor. Caroline's eyes settled into the darkness, and she saw him in profile, unbuttoning his shirt, then pulling off his T-shirt. She stared at his chest, thinking that it was hard to believe he was real.

Nervousness scattered through her.

"Come closer," he said and unbuttoned her shirt. His breath was warm on her neck. He kissed her ear and then her mouth. They moved onto the bed.

He kept kissing her. His eyes were closed, then open, and she could make out a glassiness to them. Her heart was going madly, and she felt his skin, and he undid her pants, pushed them to her ankles, and stood up to pull them off. He held her foot. "This is a pretty foot," he said.

She kissed down his chest, taking his jeans and boxer shorts down, and enclosed him in her mouth, surprised that she was doing this with him already and staying so long with his taste and shape, which to her seemed perfect.

He moved beside her and pushed down a bra strap, then the other, moving down her with his mouth, then he looked up at her and said, "Do you want me to get a condom?"

"Okay," she said, then he unfastened her bra. She couldn't help but wonder how often he unfastened a bra or reached for a condom, then her thoughts left her, and she was tangled up with him again, kissing, as he pushed inside, and he seemed to hold back until she was on top of him, until she felt as if she were falling apart and being put back together. It was everything it was supposed to be, but she didn't tell him that. How could she have told him that?

Afterward, they lay in bed, her head on his chest, and she thought of how he was moving her as he breathed. Then

Daniel began saying what he'd been thinking about Walker, and Caroline listened, was glad to listen, was glad they were finally talking about him.

Walker had said something years ago about how you could drown faster in salt water. Daniel had asked Walker if he was suicidal, and Walker thought about it, then said *at times* he was suicidal. Walker was so hard on himself, he could get depressed, sleep fifteen hours a day, not come out of his room for weeks.

Walker had painted his fingernails black his junior year, dyed his black hair even blacker. He wore an earring for a while. He made friends outside the circle of swimming, the circle of athletes. He wanted to quit all the time, but when he finally retired from swimming, when he had gotten a job and was working fifty hours a week, that was when he wanted to swim. He started going to the pool four and five times a week. He was drawn to the water. He couldn't help himself.

The Olympics were a month ago.

"I think he killed himself," Daniel said.

"I don't think he killed himself," Caroline said, sounding more confident than she felt. She had suspected it in the library that day, but it didn't make sense. Walker had seemed fine when they met. "Just because you say you've thought about suicide doesn't mean that you would do it. I've thought about it," Caroline said.

"I never have," Daniel said. He moved off the bed and began getting dressed.

"You can stay if you want," Caroline said, feeling weird, wondering if his mood change was about Walker or her.

"I can't," he said. "I have practice early."

"Oh, okay," she said, and he leaned in and kissed her quickly, and then he left.

18. | WOODEN CROSSES IN CROOKED ROWS

When the phone woke Caroline the next morning and she saw it was eight-thirty, she hoped it would be Daniel. She knew it wasn't her mother, who liked to sleep late and made it a rule of good etiquette never to call anyone before ten. If she were her mother, Caroline would have refused to answer the phone on principle.

She let the phone ring twice, giving herself a chance to sound awake. She didn't want him to regret calling her this early.

"Hello," she said, with strength and clarity, she thought.

"Oh, I'm sorry to wake you, Caroline," Daniel said.

"That's okay," she said. "I'm glad it's you."

"I didn't want to miss you. I've just decided to play a clay court tournament in Spain, so I'll be leaving for that tomorrow, and I'm on my way to hit with this guy in Mobile, then I'll be back to practice with Joseph, and later this afternoon, we could hit range balls, if you like. I find it really relaxing. Do you have any interest in doing that?"

"Sure," she said. "But I'm not any good."

"Well, good," he said. "Then you need the practice. How about I meet you at your room at four o'clock?"

"Great," she said. "I'll be ready."

After she hung up, she felt distressed that he was leaving— almost as if he was giving up on Walker, and already on her. Then she lay back on her pillow and smiled. At least he had called her, was thinking about her early in the morning. He wanted to see her again before going to Spain. Then, reflecting on the prospect of golf, she stopped smiling.

She hadn't hit a golf ball since she was in high school, and rarely then. She never much liked to do anything she couldn't be superior at. A story her father liked to tell was about her first attempt at hitting a range ball when she was six. Her father had wrapped himself around her, showing her the stance, the grip, with his hands over hers, and then the swing. Then he stood back and watched her. And when she completely missed the ball, she dropped the club and looked at him with tears in her eyes, saying, "I didn't do it vewy well." Maybe she'd had trouble with her Rs, she thought, but her grammar was spot on.

Her father had a beautiful swing. So did her grandfather. And so did Daniel, of course. And the sound of his contact was as pure as his follow-through, as pure as the arc of his ball sailing over the fairway toward a white church showing through the trees. But her swing wasn't too embarrassing. She remembered the grip her father had shown her. It was relaxing after all, she thought. Each of them with a basket of balls, hitting at their own pace. A couple of times she made a divot and saw Daniel smile. They spoke only on occasion, smiling more than speaking, and it was as if they'd known each other comfortably forever.

Sometimes she didn't believe in an afterlife, then sometimes she did. Sometimes she felt the presence of her father and her grandfather. They could have orchestrated her meeting with Daniel. It was a nice thought. Her grandfather would have done it so that through her he could play golf again at his favorite place. Maybe it was the church she was driving toward that prompted these calm feelings, or maybe it was the swarm of delicate, slow-flying, orange-and-black insects hovering over the fairway, which Daniel said were love bugs, so called because they were always mating, especially in flight, oblivious to everything but each other.

As they hit the last of their balls, the sunset glowed orange through the trees.

"That was great," Daniel said. "That was what I needed."

"Me too," she said, feeling a tinge of disappointment, looking at their empty baskets and the other empty baskets down the range. She wouldn't see him tomorrow, or for a few days after, and maybe not ever again. "Do you know when you'll be coming back?"

"The finals are on September thirtieth," he said, then shrugged with a smile. "Hopefully, not sooner than that."

Caroline hoped not sooner either. She wanted him to prove Nick Bollettieri wrong.

She recalled that she was leaving on October second, and her mother was coming on September thirtieth. That might give her and Daniel one more night together.

He carried the clubs as they walked back to his car, following a golf-cart path rippled by the roots of nearby trees, mostly magnolias and pines. He set the clubs in his trunk and shut it, then pointed in the direction of the road or to a meadow beyond it. "Let's walk over there," he said. "I want to show you something." He took her hand, and as they crossed the road, she saw white stones rising out of the grass.

"It's a Confederate cemetery," he told her.

"Oh," she said. She'd always been hushed by cemeteries.

A historical marker stood at the entrance, and Caroline stopped to read it, discovering that the Grand Hotel had served as a hospital for wounded Confederate soldiers from the Battle of Vicksburg, and those who were buried here at Confederate Rest Cemetery, more than three hundred, had died while in the hospital. The last statement—that the records of the soldiers had been destroyed in the hotel fire of 1869, causing the identities of those buried to be lost—made her draw her hand away from Daniel's to wipe her eyes. She hoped Walker would be found, or would just appear, like the delinquent youth he'd once been, that she'd once been. Or that if he hit his head on something and came out of the water with amnesia, he would live a long happy life as someone else.

She wandered to the graves. Daniel hung back, and she was glad, because now she was really crying, at the sight of the pitiful commemorative wooden crosses lined in crooked rows, because some had rotted at their base and were leaning or lying down.

She wiped her hands on her shorts and looked away, at three cannons, at a picket of cedar trees, at a few graves on the perimeter, where other soldiers were buried, their identities not lost but marked on marble blocks and broken slabs. She walked over to them, but they didn't say much—only name, rank, division number, dates of birth and death. She thought of Walker and his swim meet stats, and looked at Daniel, who was sitting on a wrought-iron bench under the cedars.

She sat next to him, leaning close to him, and he put his arm around her. Through the trees that backed the driving range, the sun was so low it looked as if it could catch the ground on fire, with the immediate air around them darkening to an almost tangible amber liquid.

She knew what her father would say to her now. "If you think to yourself that you'd like to be buried in a place, then you probably ought to live there." He was buried in Tulsa. She had been to his grave twice.

"Caroline," Daniel said.

"Yes?" she said.

"The Mobile side of the bay reopened today," he said, "but there's still so much debris in the water. Our side probably won't open for another few days. That's delaying any search for him."

Caroline nodded, wondering if that was why she hadn't seen or heard any follow-up story in the news since the one article.

"So his father would like to talk with you, if that's all right."

"What about?" she said, and turned to see Daniel better, but maybe she turned too quickly, or the prospect of talking to a grieving parent frightened her, and she lost her balance and grabbed his arm to steady herself.

"Are you okay?"

She briefly closed her eyes. "I just get a little dizzy sometimes. It's nothing." She tried to smile.

"Are you sure?" he asked.

She nodded and let go of his arm. "I'm fine. I have a little vertigo, that's all." She nodded again and felt herself blush from embarrassment. "So his father wants to speak to me?"

"Yeah, what you told the police, what you told me—he'd like to hear it himself. You'll probably get a call in a day or so.

Really, I think he just wants to meet you. It's looking more and more like you were the last person to see Walker alive."

"Well, sure," she said. "I'll do that."

"Thanks," he said, and kissed her forehead, like her father used to do.

PART
FOUR

19. | WHITE HOUSE WITH
BLACK SHUTTERS

"Caroline, this is Tom Galloway. I believe Daniel may have mentioned to you that I would call."

"Yes," said Caroline, standing to speak, too nervous to sit.

"I appreciate your willingness to talk with me. Our house is three doors south of the hotel. It's white with black shutters and cypress shingles. You can't miss it. There's no address marked from the back side, how you'll be coming from the beach. The third house. What time is good for you?"

"Anytime," she said, scrambling for a pen and a hotel pad to jot down his directions.

"Well," he said, "let's see. Tomorrow's Saturday. How about eleven o'clock? Eleven o'clock tomorrow morning?"

"Sure, that's fine," she said.

"Good," he said. "My wife and I thank you. Tomorrow at eleven. The third house. You can't miss it."

"Okay, see you then," she said.

"Good, see you then," he said.

Caroline hung up, then lay down on her bed, feeling sick. She looked at the clock. She waited until it was dark, and then she put on what she'd worn yesterday at the driving range and the Confederate cemetery, what she had taken off afterward in her room with Daniel. She'd been happy to be with him again, and he'd seemed happy to be with her. She even felt that when he left he wanted to say more to her than what he said, which was, "I'll call you." But then, because he didn't say more, she began to have the fearful feeling she would never see him again. She didn't tell him what she was feeling. She simply kissed him goodbye and wished him luck.

She went outside to see if she could find the Galloways' house, walking along the beach, past the point where she had first seen Walker, then past the point where she had spoken to him and shaken his hand, to the third house beyond a picket fence and a long lawn. A white house, a stately white house, with black shutters and cypress shingles, which she guessed were there but couldn't see. And beside it, in the shadows of shrubs and trees, a small white guesthouse.

Her sleep was restless that night. Again and again, despite waking, she dreamed what she always dreamed of her father, that he was alive but was going to die. There was nothing to be done. She knew it. Her father knew it. As if once life followed a certain order, it couldn't be reordered. Not even in dreams.

After breakfast, she watched television, but didn't really watch, thinking rather of her clothes, what to wear. She wanted Mr. and Mrs. Galloway to know that if their son had died, then the last person he had met and befriended—that was how she had grown to consider it—was at least a respectable person, which said something noble of him one final time.

When she passed through the open gate of the picket fence, wearing her black pants and white linen shirt, which had been dry-cleaned, she saw in the yard what she couldn't see last night—a rope swing hanging from one of the limbs of a live oak—and thought of a photograph, her favorite of her father and her, when he was pushing her. The swing hung from a tree in their yard, though not from a tree as big as this one, and Caroline's father would push her and she'd always ask him to make her go higher, and in this picture she had pink sunglasses on, though they would soon fall off, and her white-blond hair was flying all around her, and she was not afraid of movement or of anything.

Crossing the lawn, she saw a covered motorboat tucked beneath trees that she hadn't seen last night either, and crepe myrtle blossoms lying wilted in the grass, splashes of blackening red and dingy white. Her heart raced as she approached the guesthouse, with its columns and tall door and windows, and she wondered if the Galloways had chosen the design to match their son's height, hoping all along that he would someday return to live at home again and would need such a door to walk through. Barely visible through one window, she saw brass knobs of a dresser, but she didn't look in the window for long, in case Mr. and Mrs. Galloway were watching.

She debated whether to go around to the front door or to cross the driveway and knock on the back door. She decided on the back door, and only after she knocked and was waiting in silence, when her fear left her for the briefest moment and she almost believed that her grandfather would appear to let her in, did she realize why she'd chosen the back way. That was where she would have gone to be let in at her grandfather's—his white house with black shutters, like this white house with black shutters and with almost the same guesthouse.

Then a man much taller than her grandfather but just as neat appeared and waved at her through the glass and opened the door.

"Caroline," he said, reaching to shake her hand, and its size matched Walker's.

"Mr. Galloway, I'm so terribly sorry we have to meet like this." She had rehearsed this line.

He nodded, letting go of her hand, then stepping back and motioning her in. "Please," he said.

She followed him to a natural-colored solid-wood table in a white kitchen.

"Would you like some coffee or tea or anything, Caroline?" he asked.

"Water would be great, thanks," she said. She sat down, and thinking she heard footsteps in the house to her left, she looked in that direction, into a broad living room with a cathedral ceiling, a hardwood floor, a Persian rug, bookshelves lining an entire wall.

Mr. Galloway set a glass of ice water in front of her and sat down across from her with a cup of black coffee. Then, from the living room, Walker's mother came into view. She was almost as tall as her husband, but gaunt and grief-stricken and holding herself as though she might feel cold. She stopped at the edge of the kitchen and nodded to Caroline.

"Hi," Caroline said meekly.

"I'm Walker's mother," she said and took hurried steps toward Caroline and hugged her. She was so thin she almost wasn't there beneath her clothes, only a taut line of hard bone. "It's nice to meet you," she said into Caroline's ear.

Caroline was too horror-struck and humbled to move

quickly enough to return the hug before Mrs. Galloway stepped back, holding herself again and shaking her head.

"Thank you," she told Caroline, her voice breaking, then turned and walked back through the living room, out of sight.

"Yesterday," said Mr. Galloway in a hushed tone, "I had to take her to the hospital. She hasn't been eating or sleeping, and yesterday morning she collapsed, passed out right here on the floor," he said, turning in his chair to point behind him at the space in front of the kitchen sink. "She was given an I.V. and something to help her sleep. This is very hard."

"I want to help you if I can," said Caroline. "I can't think of anything I didn't already tell Detective Bowers or Daniel, but I can tell you exactly what I remember."

Mr. Galloway nodded, looking at her with Walker's dark, intense eyes. Caroline took a drink of water. Mr. Galloway sipped his coffee. Then Caroline began.

She was calmer telling the story to him than she thought she would be. Maybe because he didn't interrupt her with questions as Detective Bowers and Daniel had. Or maybe because she liked him, as she had immediately liked his son. Mr. Galloway's gentleness reminded her of her father. Not until she'd finished did he fold his arms on the tabletop, hunch his shoulders, and ask his first question.

"Walker actually said, 'Today's a good day for a swim'?"

"Yes, sir," she said. "I asked him if he was really going to swim in the water, and he said, 'Yeah,' or 'Sure. Today's a good day for it.' I'm positive."

"Oh, I know you are," he said. He smiled a smile of disappointment or bewilderment, then lowered his eyes to the table. "A body was found in the bay a couple of days ago. A forensics team came out, went out to the guesthouse, where Walker's been staying, and collected fingerprints and hair strands for

DNA. We found out yesterday it wasn't our son. Was some poor man who'd drowned two or three months ago." He looked up at Caroline and shook his head. "I don't honestly believe my son could drown. I don't believe, for him, it's physically possible. Caroline, there is some good explanation for this yet, I know."

"There may be," she said. "I'm hopeful."

"He didn't take flight or anything like that," he said. "There's been no activity on his credit cards and no cash withdrawals, and his passport is still out there in his dresser drawer. And I know that when the eastern shore opens up today and they start dragging the bay, they're not going to find him. There is some good explanation for this, Caroline." He pushed his chair back. "Let me show you something," he said, and he waved for her to follow him into the living room.

He took a small trophy from the mantel and showed it to her. It was the generic type she'd seen a million of—a plastic gold athlete mounted to a marble stand, with a peeling brass nameplate.

"We've got hundreds packed away in storage," he told her, "but this is his very first, when he was just five." He set it back on the mantel and pointed at the framed photo beside it, which Caroline had seen in her research. It was Walker as a young teenager eating from a bag of chips, with his goggles pushed up on his forehead. "That's a boy *and* a man driven by the talent and ambition God gave him. He was such a happy child, and happy when he was swimming."

Mr. Galloway reminded Caroline of her own father, his love and belief in his child. Tears came into her eyes, and to stop herself from crying, she looked away. At nothing, or noticing nothing, until her eyes focused on a photograph of a bald eagle, its wings spread out over its nest. At the bottom, it said LAND BETWEEN THE LAKES. Then Mr. Galloway turned from the mantel, so Caroline did the same, and she saw him looking at the television, then at the sofa.

"We watched the Olympics together, every bit of it, right there, like old times," he said, not looking at Caroline but still looking at the sofa. "He had a good job, but a grueling job, at a bank in San Francisco. Everyone out there, and here, too, is looking for somebody like Walker. He has a degree from Stanford, you know. But he decided to quit that job. Said he wanted to come back home, that he could get a job in Mobile, or with his connections, he could work at home. He made out quite well with his stock options during the dot-com boom, and he'd been talking about looking for a place of his own on the bay. He was just taking a break between jobs."

Caroline nodded. *Just like I am,* she thought.

"He moved back just last month, right before the twenty-eighth Olympiad, and we watched it all, right there, from the torch-lighting ceremony to the closing ceremony. It seemed special, with it being in Athens this year."

He glanced at Caroline, and she smiled. "That's nice," she said.

"And let me tell you this, Caroline," he said, "that Michael Phelps, he's a great swimmer, don't get me wrong, but my Walker, in his day, was every bit as good. He just didn't get the breaks that Phelps got, and you've got to get the breaks, have your best times when they matter most, and not give up because you don't. And Walker didn't give up. Oh, he'd get down sometimes, but that's the mark of a competitor. He always wanted more than what he'd accomplished. He came in third at the Olympic trials in '92, and he felt like he might as well have come in last. If you're third, you can't go, even though with that same time, he would have earned a bronze medal at the actual Olympics. But he kept going. He was the NCAA champ his senior year at Stanford. Then he made another run for the '96 Olympics, got close again at the trials. So I know he's going to show up."

"I think so, too," she said.

Mr. Galloway nodded to himself, staring at the floor.

"Is something like amnesia a possibility?"

"Oh, Caroline," he said, reaching out to touch her arm, almost giddy, "that's what I wonder." He turned and motioned behind him with his thumb, as if his wife were standing behind him and he was referring to her. "I've been saying that. It's a logical explanation, isn't it?"

"I think so," she said. "It happens to people, right?"

"They say it does," he said, nodding. He rested his hands on his hips.

He was a neat man, a handsome man, Caroline thought, with his golf shirt tucked into his khakis, with his thin leather belt and new tennis shoes. Then she noticed his watch for the first time, a Timex watch, silver with a white face and black numbers. He saw her looking at it.

"I like your watch," she said.

"It's an Easy Reader," Mr. Galloway said. He crooked his elbow and held his arm in front of him. "A good style for old eyes."

Caroline nodded.

"It's almost noon, Caroline," he said. "Would you like to join us for lunch?"

"Oh, Mr. Galloway," she said, "that's nice of you, but I guess I should get going."

"Of course," he said, taking a step and motioning that it was okay for her to begin walking toward the door. "I hope, after the hurricane and everything else you've been through, you won't hesitate to return to Point Clear."

"It's a lovely place," she said.

"It is," he said. He opened the door for her, but she didn't want to pass through. She stopped and gave him a quick hug, and he gingerly patted her on the back.

"Daniel is Walker's best friend from childhood, you know," he said. "Daniel's a good man, a fine competitor himself."

Caroline nodded and stepped outside.

"Thank you, Caroline," he said.

She nodded again, waved, then walked on, crossing the driveway, hearing the door behind her shut, passing the guesthouse. She made it halfway across the lawn, trying not to look in the direction of the tree swing, until she couldn't hold back any longer and sobbed.

The watch. She believed she would have made it without breaking down, if it wasn't for Mr. Galloway's watch.

For as long as she could remember, her father had carried an old Timex, silver with a white face and black numbers, attached to only half a black strap, essentially making a wristwatch into a pocket watch. It was a good cheap watch that never stopped working, so he loved it. He wouldn't have any other. So when he lost it while playing golf at Southern Hills, he had the greenskeepers searching the course for hours. When it was finally found and offered to him as if it were a mouse being held by its tail, the story went, he was unfazed and proudly took it. Now it sat in her jewelry box back in New York, perpetually telling the time until she wound it too tight, just days after he died, and the silver crown came off and it stopped working.

20. | THE SKY AND A SEAGULL

Caroline was still crying when she got back to her room. She could not stop herself, and didn't want to. She cried for every reason she could think of, until finally she dissolved into her bed and went to sleep. When she woke up, she ordered room service (back to jambalaya pasta), watched television while she ate, then fell asleep again.

The next morning was Sunday morning, a typical Sunday morning—quiet all around, which seemed eerie. Too quiet. As if the rebuilding were already complete. As if, perhaps, there had never been a hurricane. But just a week ago she had seen the article in the newspaper about Walker's disappearance.

She went to her purse and pulled out the clipping, then carried it to bed with her and reread it. Surely if she read and reread and thought and rethought, it would be like the way she was beginning to see Mr. and Mrs. Galloway in Walker's features if she stared at his picture long enough. Surely it was a matter of just the right perspective—if she stepped closer or stepped far enough back, the answer would be revealed.

She also thought and rethought of Daniel. She wanted to call him, to tell him about her meeting with Mr. Galloway. She had his cell phone number but wasn't sure if his phone would work in Spain. She probably shouldn't call anyway. He wouldn't have even started his tournament yet. She imagined he would be there somewhere in Spain, she hadn't even asked where, practicing with other players, getting prepared for the first day on Monday.

She opened up her laptop, turned it on, and figured out how to connect to the Internet by phone by finding access numbers from Mobile that would work.

Mr. Galloway had mentioned that Walker had come close but failed in another run for the Olympics, in '96. She wanted to learn what had happened. She had missed any reference to it before. She searched in different ways with different search terms on different search engines. Her laptop was much slower than the one at the library.

What she found out, with patience, was that Walker had come in sixth at the trials, which to her seemed unbelievable, especially when she saw he had gone into them being ranked #2 in the world in the 200-meter backstroke. She read that if the event had been the 100-meter backstroke instead of the 200-meter backstroke, he would have won. Caroline sat back from the screen and shut her eyes, imagining Walker's eyes from the picture in the clipping, wondering what he was thinking, what he was seeing with those intensely penetrating, vulnerable eyes, and she wondered if somewhere in the last hundred meters he looked at his competitors, saw that he might come in third again, and, not wanting that devastation, just slowed down, so he would not come anywhere close to third, to coming once again as close as you can get to the Olympics without going. As far as Caroline could tell, that was the last race he ever swam.

She decided to search the word "backstroke." She was determined to learn how to swim it, and she was determined to write about Walker, not in a diaristic way, as notes for some vaguely possible novel in the future, but from his point of view, the main character of a novel very soon to be in progress. She read about the mechanics of the stroke, how to rotate your shoulders, kick your legs, how to turn at the wall. She copied the article onto her hard drive. It all looked amazingly difficult, to do and to write about, but she wanted to try. She felt she needed to try.

Then she checked her e-mail, and she was surprised that among the junk mail she had a real one—from her mother.

> *Dear Caroline,*
>
> *David and I will be arriving at the Grand Hotel about four o'clock on Thursday, September 30. I will call you when we are all checked in. Please plan on eating dinner with us that night, and afterward, you and I could spend some time together, maybe just in your room or we could take a walk, whatever you'd like to do. I can't wait to see you. It's been too long for your mother to go without seeing her little girl.*
>
> *Love,*
> *Mom*

At that moment, Caroline felt a warmth for her mother. Maybe it was from meeting Walker's mother the day before, she wasn't sure, but she wrote this back:

Sounds good.
Love,
Caroline

It was hard for her to believe that she hadn't seen her mother in over a year.

She was missing Daniel. She got out of her e-mail and searched for the draw to Daniel's tournament in Spain, but couldn't find anything more than that there was a challenger tournament in Seville. That made her feel better, just to have some connection to where he was, some knowledge, however slight.

She decided to call Emma. She called her own apartment and heard her own voice mail, so she hung up and called Emma's cell.

Emma answered, and it was obvious from the road noise that she was in a car.

"Hey," Caroline said.

"Hey, I've been meaning to call you."

"How are you?"

"Well, truthfully," Emma said, "not great. Anthony almost just killed us with one of his one-eyed turns. He sideswiped someone. Totally his fault. The police came. It was a mess. So it's taking us now like three hours to get into Manhattan."

"Oh, I'm sorry," Caroline said. "I'm glad you're all right, though."

"Yeah, we're fine. What's up?"

"Well, I wanted to tell you about this guy that I met," said Caroline.

"So have you had sex with him yet?"

"Well," Caroline said, wishing she would've gotten a chance to brag that Daniel was single and had no kids and was a professional tennis player. But then she smiled. "We've had sex twice now," she said, "and it's been amazing both times. One time at night and once in the day."

"So once drunk and once sober," Emma said, then laughed.

Caroline thought about it and, realizing this was true, said, "But we've had three dates."

"That sounds really good. Three dates is a lot, especially in such a short amount of time."

"That's what I think," said Caroline. "So tell me, how's the film going?"

"Oh, editing's slow," Emma said. "I've got so much footage, I could go a million ways, not to mention all the B-roll to consider." Car horns blared close by, and Caroline imagined Emma and Anthony sitting in traffic smoking cigarettes.

"I know you have to go. I just wanted to tell someone."

"Oh, sure," Emma said. "I completely understand. I'll talk to you later. I think this sounds promising."

"Thanks," Caroline said. "Bye."

After she set the receiver down, guilt nagged at her, then gradually consumed her. She had told Emma about Daniel but had said nothing about Walker. But what would she have said?

Miriam had a client who'd written a novel in which the first chapter was titled "How It Ended." It began with a murder, and the rest of the book was about what had happened leading up to it. Caroline liked that structure, that you could begin at the end, and that by doing so, you could make the vague, loose ties of any beginning much more meaningful to follow.

For the next three days, while Daniel was living the life of a professional tennis player and Emma the life of a film director, Caroline lived the life of a writer. She got on the Internet each day to read all she could about swimming, until finally she decided she had to try the backstroke herself.

She kicked off her shoes and walked tentatively over the shifting sand to the lazy surf of the bay, feeling the crushed shells, then the muddy bottom between her toes as her feet sank, then the bottom hardened into ridges, so that she felt as if she were walking down stairs. A little girl whose mother lay on a lawn chair reading a magazine followed Caroline closely.

"It's green!" the little girl said. "It's green!" The water, smelling fishier than normal, was a dark murky green in front of them, then brown, then blue and silver farther out. "It's scary!" the little girl said. "What are those black things touching me?"

"I think it's seaweed," Caroline said. She was not used to talking to children, so she talked to her as if she were an adult. "I've read there may be little jellyfish floating around us, supposedly the harmless kind, but I'm afraid, too. It's shallow, though, and that's good."

The little girl pushed her mask on top of her head and started walking back to her mother.

Caroline continued walking into the water, and though the bottom had leveled out, with the surface undulating just above her waist, she was still afraid, hoping that the slight tingling she felt on her arms and legs was harmless jellyfish brushing against her and not a crab, not a shark. She had seen a shark only about a hundred yards out at dusk the night before, its frightening fin clearly visible. She didn't want to think about Walker and sharks. Daniel had told her there were only sand sharks in the bay, only nippers, not dangerous.

The farther she went into the water, the stronger she felt, until she lay on her back and began her terrible backstroke. She looked at the sky and a seagull and got disoriented. She flipped herself over and tasted salt water. But she was glad for the experience. Clearly she wasn't Walker, but clearly she wasn't herself either.

She didn't go to Celtic Twilight Hour on Wednesday, even though Joseph called to remind her. She told him she was writing. One of Miriam's clients had told Caroline that you had to give up things if you wanted to write. If someone asked you to a movie or for a drink, you would have to learn to say no, and not to feel bad. To write you needed time, uninterrupted time.

By late Wednesday night, she had finally finished the first chapter. And though it was technically a novel she was writing, it felt more like nonfiction. She would have to change the names later. Caroline hadn't written anything since NYU, so she was feeling good about herself when the phone rang and it was Daniel.

"I'm not calling too late, am I?"

"Oh, no," Caroline said. "Hi, I'm so happy to hear your voice."

"I'm happy to hear your voice, too," he said. "You have a sexy phone voice."

"Really?" she said, then began to feel embarrassed. "How'd you do in the tournament?"

"Not too great," he said. "I lost in the second round."

"I'm sorry," she said. And though she felt bad for him, she was excited that she would be seeing him soon.

"It's okay," he said. "I lost to this same guy I've been losing to for years. You know, being a tennis player is kind of like being in a traveling circus. We travel all over the world, and wherever we go, it's the same dudes all the time."

Caroline thought she heard an announcement in the background, like a boarding call. He was at the airport. "I can't wait to see you," she said.

"Well, I hate to tell you this," Daniel said, "but I really need to play this tournament in France. It's a hard-court tournament, which is really my best surface, and I think I can win it. I need the money, Caroline, and the points, and it starts Friday, so I'm flying over there, so I'll have a day to practice. There are some friends of mine going over early, too. I'm sorry, I just have to go."

"That's okay," Caroline said. "I leave on Saturday. I hate I'm going to miss you before I leave."

"I know," he said. "But I'd like to come see you sometime in New York, if that'd be okay?"

"Sure," she said. "I'd like that."

"Well, I hate to say goodbye, but I have to. My flight's boarding. My friends are waving for me to come on already."

"Oh, okay," she said, feeling defeated. "Bye," she said.

"Caroline," he said. "Will you give me your address and phone number in New York? I can write it down right now."

It was polite of him to ask, so she gave him the information.

"But I'll try to call you before then."

Afraid she would never talk to him again, she persisted. This was something she had to say. "I met Walker's father," she said.

"I know," Daniel said. "He told me. I'm sorry but my friends are really waving at me. I just have to go. Bye, Caroline."

"Bye," she said.

She hung up the phone and sat on the edge of her bed for a long time. Then she reached for her chapter and read through it again.

21. | Chapter One:
HOW IT ENDED

He stood at the waterline, letting the bay of his youth rock against his ankles, then stretched his arms behind his back until they bowed and loosened. He didn't think of the flecks of gray in his black hair. He was thirty, but he could have been fourteen.

"Excuse me," he heard, faint words on the wind, so faint he might have only been remembering them, but he turned and saw he was not alone. A blond woman, his age, stood on the beach behind him, someone he had never seen before, so he smiled

"Doesn't the water look beautiful?" he said.

"It looks murky, but I suppose there's beauty in that," she said, and he liked that

she shared his sense of the world. "Are you
going to swim in it?" she asked.

"Sure," he said. "Today's a good day for it."

He thought of telling her that he had swum
after other hurricanes and tropical storms. He
liked to witness rugged beauty tiring out. She
was quiet, and he liked that about her. She
swept hair from her eyes and looked at him,
then looked at the water. She, too, he thought,
was drawn to the water.

"I'm staying at the Grand Hotel," she said.
"I was supposed to evacuate, but I didn't.
You're the only one who knows where I am."

"So you made it," he said. He was happy for
her. She, too, was a risk-taker.

"I made it," she said, appearing about to cry
and walking closer. It seemed she wanted to
introduce herself, so he walked closer, and as he
did, she told him her name. Caroline. She seems
like me, he thought, shaking her hand, or holding
it, or enclosing it more than shaking it.

"My name is Walker," he said. He'd stayed up
all night during the hurricane, but he felt
fully awake, though he could see she was red-
eyed from sleeplessness.

"So, do you live around here, or are you on
vacation, too?" she asked.

"My parents live a few houses down," he
said. "And for now, anyway, I live in their
guesthouse." As he spoke of it, he thought of
his parents vacationing in the Land Between the
Lakes in Kentucky. It was probably too early

for them to have seen a bald eagle. They were bird-watchers, his parents. They wanted him to hurry up already and apply for a job in Mobile—that was probably where he'd have to work—but he'd still live in Point Clear and get his own place on the bay. It had to be somewhere on the bay.

"You didn't evacuate either?" she asked. She seemed delighted not to have toughed it out alone, and he realized as he answered her that he was delighted by that, too.

"So we're both not supposed to be here," he said, thinking that he liked how she smiled. He could see by her joints she was comfortable with land. He hoped he wasn't staring at her too long.

"I think I'm going back in and try to sleep," she said.

He nodded. "That's good," he said. "I'm going to do that soon myself."

"That's good," she said, nodding, too, and turned away.

He watched her short stride, the angle of her instep, and realized that she was slightly pigeon-toed, just enough to have had a chance to make use of it, as he had made use of being double-jointed by being a swimmer, and he hoped she'd made use of her flaw. He'd heard from tennis players who were friends of his that it could help someone with balance. He hoped she'd been a tennis player. Then he watched her turn toward him again.

"It was nice to meet you," she said.

He tilted his head down, bent his knees, his body, until he was shaped like an S, so that he wasn't six foot six but five foot something and seeing her at eye level. "Maybe we'll meet each other again, Caroline," he told her.

"I'd like to," she said.

Walker unstuck his feet from the silky bog of mud and began to walk into the water and was reminded of a million swim meets, all the crowded pools during warmup. That water, though clearer, was almost this water, rocking, thrashing. The sky vanished, all memories, all thoughts, all sounds. He focused only on the water gradually rising higher along his legs.

"Please, be careful," he heard, and this time he believed they were remembered words—his mother's words.

"I've swum in this bay a million times," he said, not knowing he was speaking aloud.

At waist-deep, he turned and lay leisurely back, and it was as if he had sandpapered his back the way he used to do his palms, because he felt the water eddy under him with great sensitivity. He'd never known the water completely, he thought. Never completely. No one did.

His arm strokes were slow, and his leg strokes weren't much faster, though he knew that as he went farther and faced more turbulence, he would have to adjust, reduce drag, increase rotation. Even so, at this pace or close to this pace, he could backstroke six *miles. At least six. On a calm day, he could push sixteen.*

He relished that this was no warmup, this was no practice, there was no pace clock. No walls to interrupt his rhythm. He could stretch out his stroke and be the kid he was when he swam out into the bay for the first time. Or the kid he was later when he didn't stop, when he kept going, until he reached Gaillard Island and sat on the beach laughing. Or the kid he was even later, at the age of twelve, when he didn't stop at Gaillard Island but kept going, dodging boats, until he reached the opposite shore and, too tired to swim back, called a cab.

With his eyes closed, he imagined the map of Mobile Bay, which he had always seen as the relaxed foot of a swimmer. The heel at Bon Secour, the toes at Mobile, the arch at Point Clear. He imagined he could pass Gaillard Island and Middle Bay Lighthouse, that he could reach the ankle, the deepest waters. He imagined he could almost reach the gulf, and on today's faster current, he might. He knew it wouldn't have been possible today, but reaching Middle Bay Lighthouse—something he'd done for the first time when he was eleven, then again later, countless times, during high school and once, the last time, during college one summer, when he was younger and more fit—would be, and that would be challenge enough.

Despite the arrhythmic movement of the bay, he was pinwheeling with ease and grace, and decided to speed up his strokes. He was happiest when he was swimming. He'd forgotten that sometimes, but he didn't forget that now.

He could have been swimming down a waterfall. The currents coursed around him so thoroughly they could have been passing through him, and he thought that today he could know the water completely. Somehow, without effort, he'd avoided the hurricane's debris, wherever it was. He felt the bay's hidden order and adjusted to the chop and swell with perfect timing. He didn't fight the waves but dolphin-kicked under them when he couldn't swim through them. With his eyes closed, he could be passing by overturned boats and trees and not know it, and he didn't want to know it. He only wanted to concentrate on swimming while his parents were away, while the bay was still closed, before even the Coast Guard patrolled.

He felt the currents breaking ahead of him and readied himself for what was coming, then suddenly felt something in his head shift, and his stroke collapsed, and he found himself clinging to something cold and sharp but solid and stationary, and holding his head.

He tried to open his eyes but was too dizzy. He waited a moment, without panic, then tried again, and slowly, with his head throbbing, he saw that what he was clinging to was the steel base of an overturned beacon. He touched the back of his head, then checked his hand. There was some blood, but not much blood.

There was a gash in his head, but it was a small gash.

Once the spinning in his head slowed to an acceptable rate, he let go of the beacon, sailed out from it, closing his eyes, and began churning his arms and hips faster than before. Before long he'd forgotten the pain.

There should be nothing ahead of him now but open water. And, eventually, Middle Bay Lighthouse. An elegant hexagonal structure, painted white with black shutters.

His body and his knowledge of the bay told him that he had swum three miles. He was halfway.

The hurricane last night had inspired him, and he wished to live up to it. He'd moved from California back home to Point Clear out of the hope that this would happen, that something somewhere would inspire him, something out of the past or the present. It didn't matter. He was living in both.

He couldn't be tired yet. He couldn't be this out of shape. This couldn't be his body. His body had never failed him.

He had failed his body, by eating the wrong foods, drinking the wrong drinks, by not training enough. But his body had never failed him.

What he had to do was ignore the pain in his head, this lethargy, this desire to quit and sleep. He felt soreness and exhaustion coming to his muscles, but he knew he had one more mile of strength in them, and when he reached Middle Bay Lighthouse, rising out of the water on slender steel pilings crisscrossed with cables, he would climb the cables, as though he were climbing three beacons stacked on top of one another, pausing in the crook of each X to hold the cold steel and catch his breath, and when he had reached the deck and flung himself over the railing, where a lighthouse keeper in the early 1900s had kept a cow for fresh milk, he'd break inside, if the hurricane hadn't already broken the windows for him. Maybe there would be a blanket inside, and he'd take a nap before swimming back.

He didn't let himself slow. He was calm and steady and fast, reciting the Olympic Creed to the timing of his strokes:

> The most important thing in the Olympic Games is not to win but to take part, just as the most important thing in life is not the triumph but the struggle. The essential thing is not to have conquered but to have fought well.

But he was slowing, steadily slowing, and trailing blood that could only be smelled, not seen, not even felt. If his eyes were open, he would have known that the lighthouse was no more than two hundred yards away. But he was reciting, he was stretching, he was kicking, he was breathing. And when he breathed his last breath, and his head slipped under the surface, he still believed he was breathing and that the air had never tasted better.

22. | THE FLOWER GARDEN

"Caroline, it's your mother."

"Are you here?"

"We're here. All checked in and ready to see you. We're in the spa building on the third floor, overlooking the harbor. Room 1316."

"Well, I'm in the spa building overlooking the harbor, too, on the *fourth* floor. Room 1418. Hang up and go outside on the balcony. I bet I can wave to you."

Caroline walked out onto the balcony, leaned out, looked down, and got completely dizzy seeing her mother.

"Caroline," her mother said, seeing clearly what had happened, "I'll come up to you."

Caroline took small careful steps back inside and lay on the bed, keeping her head still, until her mother knocked. Then she got up and answered the door.

Her mother was wearing red linen pants and a red-and-white striped shirt, something Caroline would have never worn, but it looked very good. "Hi, Mom," Caroline said.

"Oh, hi," her mother said and hugged her, then began crying. "Oh, Caroline, I can't believe we're here."

"Me either," Caroline said.

"Your father and I were really in love here," her mother said, walking inside the room, looking around. "I believe you were conceived in this hotel."

"Not in this building," Caroline said. "It's new, you know, wasn't even close to being here when you were here."

Her mother was unfazed. "All we ever had to say to remind us of what we had was 'Point Clear.' We ended lots of arguments just by one of us speaking those two words."

The story sounded somewhat familiar to Caroline, though now remarkable. She was glad that her parents were once really in love, that they fell in love here.

"You know," her mother said, looking through the glass of the balcony doors, "the week before your father died, we were outside working in the yard. It was on a Saturday in springtime, and we were working in the flower garden. Oh, did that yard look beautiful!" She turned and smiled at Caroline. "The azaleas were blooming just a bright, bright pink, and the jonquils had bloomed, and we had just gone to the nursery and were planting blue pansies. I was outside in work clothes, Bermuda shorts and a T-shirt, and he was wearing that straw hat that he liked to mow the yard in and sometimes play golf in, with the wide brim that would keep out the sun. Then all of a sudden he just grabbed me and kissed me with so much passion and said, 'You know, I love you. I just love you.' "

Her mother clasped her hands at her chest. "Well, it just surprised me, you know, and I said, 'Well, Paul, I love you, too.'"

"We stayed like that a moment," her mother continued, "just staring at each other, then I thought that it would be a good time to ask him to go with me to the garden show the next day, on Sunday. I knew you wouldn't have wanted to go. You really loved flowers as a little girl, but as a teenager they didn't interest you much."

"They do now," Caroline said.

"Really?" her mother said and smiled.

"Did you go to the garden show?" Caroline asked.

"We did go, and we had just a wonderful time, but he didn't want to go at first. At first he said, 'No, I don't think so.' But then he thought about it some more and decided that he would, that of course he would take me." She took a deep breath and shifted her eyes slightly away from Caroline. "You know," she said, now in a softer tone, "I always felt that I had loved him more than he loved me, until that day in the flower garden."

Her mother was in her own world now. Her eyes had stopped blinking. She didn't even look conscious, somewhere between living and dying, just remembering.

"That's a nice story," Caroline said. "You've never told me that story. And that happened just a week before he died?"

"And on a Sunday, too," her mother said.

Caroline nodded but didn't quite know what she meant.

Her mother glanced at Caroline, then turned back to the balcony doors and opened them, as if to let in the flowers or the birds or the bay. "Your father was so proud of his job," she said, still with her back to Caroline. "Then Phillips hired McKinsey & Company to evaluate certain management positions. It was a cost-cutting measure, to make Phillips competitive in the oil industry. So your father was fired. He had no place to go, Caroline. He felt he had no place to go."

For a moment, there was only a slight breeze passing through the room and no other sound, no other movement.

"Mom," Caroline said, "what are you talking about?" She watched her mother's shoulders lift with a breath, then fall. "You don't think he could have wrecked his car on purpose, do you?"

"What?" her mother said, appearing confused, then, appearing to understand the question now, shook her head firmly. "Oh, no, Caroline."

"Well, I didn't know. I just wondered." Caroline would have liked to have said more. She missed talking to her mother the way they used to talk before her father died.

Her mother quietly studied her. "What makes you ask that, Caroline?"

Caroline hesitated. Walker had increasingly become too private a subject for her to talk about. Yet she began to explain, surprising herself: "I met someone who didn't evacuate before the hurricane, and now he's missing."

"And you suspect he took his own life?"

"No, *I* don't," Caroline said, "but his best friend does."

Her mother looked hurt as Caroline felt hurt, so Caroline continued: "The last time anyone saw him he was swimming in the bay, and since he's a champion swimmer, I guess it's starting to look less and less like an accident."

Her mother reached for the edge of one of the doors and leaned against it. "How old was he?"

"Thirty."

Her mother shook her head. "Very sad."

"He just vanished," said Caroline. "But there was no note."

"They often don't leave one. I learned that from the grief support groups I went to. You know, so many people's lives are sad."

"That's why I asked."

"Well, your father was certainly depressed, and I worried about him, but he didn't—no, I'm positive of that."

Caroline saw her father, two hands on the wheel when he wasn't shifting, always a safe driver. He never used cruise control because of how lethargic it left you. "I'm sure you're right," she said. "I don't think he did either."

"The road was slick. He lost control. That truck driver saw it all clearly."

"It's just that car," said Caroline. "It seems so unlike Dad to get a car like that."

Her mother stood away from the door and nodded. "I was mad at first that he was going to buy it. But when he pulled into the driveway and honked and waved, so happy driving it, you said to me, 'Mom, don't say anything else mean about the car,' and I said, 'Okay, I won't.' Do you remember that?"

Caroline shook her head. "I don't."

"He wanted one of those Alfa Romeo sports cars for the longest time. But I thought it was so silly. Someone his age with a convertible. But after he lost his job, he was so down, and that car made him happy the last year of his life. He loved that car." Tears came to her eyes, and they came to Caroline's, and then her mother smiled. "No, he didn't wreck his car on purpose. For a while it saved him, it really did. He felt good again about himself. It was just a terrible, terrible accident, what happened."

Caroline wanted to sit down but didn't want to move, and began to cry, thinking of her father, and of Walker, tangling their images, feeling like she loved them both. But did she really know them? The closest she'd ever come to death was her vertigo that time in Union Square Park, before Emma's hand reached for hers. Caroline remembered calmness, as if she were drifting away to die and accepting that she was going to die. She was afraid that when her father died, he felt panic and fear. "Sometimes I think I didn't really even know him," she told her mother. "We could play tennis or cards, and sometimes he'd tell me about growing up and his neighborhood friends—where they built tree houses and forts and found arrowheads. He talked about his childhood friend Shorty Fourworth all the time. Do you remember that?"

"Oh, yeah," her mother said. "How could you forget that name! But I felt confused about him, too. I couldn't believe I was lucky enough to be married to him, but you know, sometimes he just wouldn't even talk to me. I'd try to spark up a conversation, but he just didn't want to talk to me."

Caroline nodded but didn't sympathize. She wanted to close the balcony doors. She wanted to lie down.

"David talks to me," her mother said. "You know, Caroline, it's nice to have someone who will talk to me."

Caroline felt herself growing jealous, growing mad. "You know," Caroline said, "it's not like you ever really want to talk to me, or at least not for long." She was surprised she'd said it but told herself not to stop, that she was saying what she'd been wanting to say for a long time. "David is always coming in or around or will be there soon. You haven't even visited me in New York. Why? Why not, Mom? You're going to go to the Fountain of Youth, historic homes, but don't want to see New York City. What's wrong with New York?"

"Nothing is," she said. "I could come visit you there. It's just that David and I are senior citizens now, and New York is just not a place we've wanted to go."

"And Africa is?" Caroline said. "Brussels is? That's ridiculous."

"All right, Caroline," her mother said. "You've made your point."

Caroline moved toward the bed, and she must have moved too quickly, with her mind racing. *Why couldn't he have been more careful in that car? Casey said. Caroline liked Joseph's car. It reminded her of her father's old cars. Today's a good day for it, Walker said. If you think you'd like to be buried in a place, then you probably ought to live there, her father said. I'm going to do that soon myself, Walker said. He always wanted more than what he'd accomplished, Mr. Galloway said. In Caroline's dreams, her father knew he was going to die I don't see God intervening former swimming star reported missing.* It was as if the last nine years of her life had come unwound and sent her outside of herself, falling backward, buckling to the floor.

Her mother rushed to her. "Oh, Caroline, are you all right?"

Caroline tried to stand, and her mother helped her, then guided her to the bed.

"I'll be all right," Caroline said, the spinning already slowing.

"You know," her mother said, "when you were a little girl, you never left my side. You used to grab on to my leg. My friends would kid me about it. The little girl who wouldn't let go of my knee." She smiled and walked around the bed and lay down beside Caroline, both propped up by pillows.

"And I took you to all those tennis tournaments, Caroline. We had enough money then that any tournament you wanted to play in, wherever it was, we would just go. I loved those days. Those tennis days. I was so proud of you. You were dressed in the cutest outfits, and Mother would braid your hair. Then she started braiding all the girls' hair. Remember that?"

Caroline's grandmother, whom they called Noomy, had died when Caroline was fifteen, but Caroline remembered Noomy at the hotels, little girls knocking on the door, one after another—it was a way that Caroline made friends, to have Noomy do one French braid down the middle or two French braids down the sides, sometimes tying them with ribbons or holding back the hair with little barrettes.

"Since your father died," her mother said, "you always have an edge with me. That's why I e-mailed you instead of calling before coming here. I didn't want to hear that edge on the phone."

Caroline reached for her mother's hand, soft with lotion. "I'm sorry, Mom," she said. "From now on, no edge."

"Well," her mother said, "it's normal for there to be an edge every once in a while between a mother and daughter, just not all the time. Is that a deal?"

"That's a deal," Caroline said.

"Now, Caroline," her mother said, turning and leaning in, "don't get mad."

Caroline stayed still, focusing on a sun spot on the wall. "What?"

"I invited Casey to join us tomorrow. It's been too long since we've all been together."

"All the way from Florida? For how long?"

"Just tomorrow. He's flying up just for the day."

"Oh, Mom, he doesn't want to come here. Why did you do that?"

"No, he does. He jumped at it. You know, he loves flying that little Cessna of his. I hate thinking about it, but I think he does fine in it. And he said he wanted to see you, anyway."

"He did? Really?"

"He did. This will be good for us. David's heard about a lighthouse out in the bay dating back to the eighteen hundreds. He thought it would be fun for us to take a boat out and see it together. If you think you can."

Caroline slowly turned to her. "Middle Bay Lighthouse?"

"Yes, that's the one," her mother said. She smiled, then held Caroline gently, patting her shoulder, before pushing herself out of the bed.

"I can," Caroline said.

"Good, and do you feel up to having dinner with David and me tonight? We can eat in the restaurant that faces the bay."

"Sure," Caroline said.

"Well," her mother said, "I feel exhausted, but much, much better. I'm going to go freshen up, and you do the same, then I'll call you when we're ready to go. It'll be about twenty minutes, I'd guess. Is that okay?"

"That sounds good," Caroline said. "I'm starting to get hungry."

"You actually look very thin," Caroline's mother said. "I bet you're as thin as you were in high school."

"Not quite," Caroline said.

"I bet it's close, though. Have you been playing tennis?"

"I have," Caroline said. "I've played quite a bit. There's a wonderful tennis pro here."

"Oh, good," her mother said. "I'll call you in a little while."

"Mom, you look really good, too. Beautiful, actually."

Her mother's face lit up. "Oh, well, thank you, sugar plum," she said, and that made Caroline smile.

They had dinner in the Grand Dining Room, and they ate while watching the sun set into spectacular purples and pinks. "Isn't this gorgeous?" her mother kept saying. Then David would agree. David was a nice man, older than her mother. He had an easy way about him and no edge whatsoever, as if he had learned that no edge was how to live a life.

Her mother had shrimp, David had snapper, and Caroline had chicken. As much as she loved Point Clear, she did not really care for fish. Maybe one day that would change, but it didn't have to. She thought she was changing enough.

"So, I met this guy," Caroline began, and told her mother and David as much as she could about Daniel, then having said all she wanted to say, she looked out into the darkening sky, staring out over the bay, her eyes finally resting on the thin line of flickering lights that was Mobile. Like hope itself.

Later that night, after dropping David off so he could go to bed early, Caroline and her mother walked along the hotel's path, occasionally stepping over CAUTION signs or PARDON OUR PROGRESS signs where bricks were being realigned or where a pier was being rebuilt. They walked past Walker's house, though Caroline did not tell her mother they were doing so. Her mother wanted to talk, and Caroline felt she owed it to her to listen.

Her mother talked about David. "We've seen the world together," she said, "and he's been a wonderful companion for me." Her mother explained very practically that David was dying. She was already accepting that he would die, that this would be the last of their travels. His heart was weakening; only 20 percent was functioning. The doctor had told her, "One to five years, though that seems awfully optimistic." He had an atrial fibrillation. He was fine when he was sitting, but when standing, which he would be doing a lot of tomorrow, his blood pressure could drop and cause him to fall. It'd been a week since his last fall, and her mother was afraid he was due. He wouldn't become dizzy, but he always knew when a fall was coming, and he was powerless to stop it.

David didn't want her to tell anyone, not his children or Casey or Caroline, about his illness. David was a proud man who hated pity. Even after the doctor's news, he was still saying, "I always bounce back." Caroline thought about how he was different from her father, who seemed to enjoy being sick, taking a day off from work in which he could prop up with soft pillows and watch television and eat Popsicles.

She shared her thought with her mother, and they laughed at the image. And then her mother told her, as if Caroline were a friend, "Just imagining him lying in bed like that sends sparks through me."

23. | MIDDLE BAY LIGHTHOUSE

Casey, her mother, David—they were already there, gathered closely together in a circle on the dock by a large white boat. A red-haired woman was moving about on board, in and out of the raised and enclosed pilothouse. Caroline looked at the group as she approached, at her mother wearing a yellow outfit, at David wearing a yellow shirt and khakis, and finally at Casey, not matching either one, wearing jeans and a green T-shirt with an Egyptian-looking logo that said THE WILDLIFE SOCIETY.

Caroline could hear her brother laughing, her father laughing, but could not clearly see his face yet, their father's face. She knew it would be hard to see Casey, to be around him. She knew she should want to see him, to be reminded of her father, but she didn't want to see him. Even from a distance, with his height, his sloping shoulders, how he stood, he was already an exact duplicate.

"Hi there," Caroline said, attempting to sound casual, and they all turned around.

Her brother reached out, hugging her. Then he stood back, looking at her, looking at her with his blue eyes in a fascinated way, as if he were trying to see their relation.

"How are you?" Caroline said. "How was the flight?"

He smiled at her. "I'm fine. The flight was fine. I had to take what's called the chicken route. I couldn't go the direct route over the water, so I saw a lot of hurricane damage on my way here."

Caroline nodded, but she was thinking about his small two-seater, a Cessna 150—how you would feel the turbulence all around you. She remembered riding in her father's car, how you could feel the air around you, and hear the air. She thought of hiding under the bed, of lying in the bathtub during the hurricane, how that was risky, extravagant behavior, like flying a small plane or driving an Alfa Romeo Spider.

"Okay, are we ready?" their mother said. "Caroline, did you take your pill?"

"I took two," Caroline said.

"Good, I don't want you getting sick."

Casey put his hands in his pockets and shrugged. "Mom told me what happened in New York."

Caroline nodded. "I feel better now."

"That's good," he said.

Caroline looked over at her mother, then at David, who was looking out toward the redheaded captain, with thoughts, Caroline imagined, of his old life, his first wife, and their house by the San Francisco Bay. Then she wondered if his thoughts had returned yet to the recognition of his health.

"I have to take Xanax sometimes," Casey said, and Caroline turned back to him.

"You do?" she said.

"If I have to give a presentation. Oh, yeah."

Their mother stepped closer to David, taking hold of his elbow.

"Are you ready?" her mother asked him, and he took a step toward the boat.

"Never been more ready," he said.

Casey leaned over to Caroline. "Mom dotes on him too much, don't you think?"

As they boarded the boat, the captain pointed out where the life preservers were located, but they didn't put them on. There were two bench seats in front of the pilothouse, with their mother and David paired up on one and Caroline and Casey on the other.

Casey's brown hair stayed in place as the motor left a trail of white behind them. It was the first time Caroline had seen his hair short. It always used to be somewhat long and wavy, which made him always seem like a boy.

Once beyond the mouth of the marina, they sped up on a loop around the bay, beginning on the eastern side. The water looked almost blue today, matching Casey's eyes. When Caroline was younger, she wished she had blue eyes like her father's and Casey's, but hers were green like her mother's. She looked more like her mother.

Caroline leaned in, her hair tangling around her face, and raised her voice to be heard over the wind and motor. "So what exactly do you do in the Everglades?"

"Well, I'm more of a botanist," Casey said, almost shouting. "I study rare and endangered plants." He stared off ahead of them as if studying the horizon for what might appear. "Though most of the money is in endangered species, and the big one in Florida is the Florida panther. There's been a huge effort to preserve the species. Sometimes I work on that, too."

Caroline nodded. "Sounds like important work. I'm proud of you."

He sat back and gazed at her without blinking. "In this type of research, we try to obtain blood or hair or scat samples for DNA, since it can be used to infer a variety of things." He was yelling still, because he had to, but sitting down and being this close to him, she was struck with the memory of when he yelled at her, grabbing her shoulders and shaking her, after their father's funeral. Maybe he looked like their father, but they weren't the same man.

"What do people fish for around here?" she heard David ask.

"Redfish, mostly," the captain said.

"What kind of fish are those?" David said, pointing, and Caroline and Casey looked over. Caroline had watched them before—silver flashes arcing over the water.

"Mullet, right?" Casey said, looking up at the captain.

"Mullet," she said. "They're caught using a cast net, mostly."

David nodded studiously, and Caroline's mother smiled and took his hand.

Casey leaned in to finish what he was saying about his work in the Everglades. "Genetic diversity, the thing that makes individuals different," he went on, "is the raw material of evolution and the basis for the ability of an organism to adapt to a changing environment. When populations fall, genetic variation is lost, and the next step is extinction."

She knew he was trying to impress her, and he was. Maybe he was different. Maybe he had adapted and she hadn't. Being the older sister by two years, Caroline was used to impressing *him*. A story her mother liked to tell was that when Casey was born and their mother brought him home from the hospital,

Caroline rushed in with a picture book, and though she couldn't read yet, she pretended to read it to him, making up the story as she went along, sometimes the words just gibberish.

"Hey," said Caroline, wiping her hair from her mouth, "did Mom tell you that you didn't have to go to Granddad's funeral, or did she say she wanted you to be there?"

Casey shrugged. "I wanted to go," he said. "But don't worry. We all understood why you didn't."

Caroline looked away, not sure what to think of that, and she and her mother caught sight of each other. Her mother smiled with approval, and Caroline knew why. Caroline and Casey were together. They were talking again.

"You know, Dad's funeral was tough for me," Caroline said.

"What?" said Casey.

She turned to him and spoke louder. "Dad's funeral was tough for me, you know. Tougher than it might have seemed."

Casey ran his fingers through his hair, from front to back, then left his hand on top of his head, holding it, with his elbow out. It was a familiar gesture. "I know," he said, this time without shouting, so the words were nearly too soft to be heard. "I acted crazy, didn't I? That wasn't right of me."

The boat slowed, and then stopped, slightly rocking, and David moved next to the captain, pointing at land in the distance. Caroline looked at the water, gray-blue under the clouds, and thought about Walker being lost to it. She was becoming more and more certain that his final wish had been to find the gulf and be lost in it forever. She'd thought she'd been honest in her writing, but she may have let her father's death color her perspective. If Daniel, who knew Walker better than most, and perhaps best, felt certain that he wanted to die, then he probably did.

"You know," Casey said and Caroline turned to him. "I've

always been fascinated by DNA work. It's very powerful to obtain and isolate in a test tube the very essence of life. I remember when I first extracted DNA, how it made me feel like something magical was in my hands."

She smiled at him. She could tell he didn't want to stop talking. As long as they weren't talking about their father, he was happy to talk, but maybe they were always talking about their father. "Nowadays," he said, "we can take it and manipulate it at the molecular level, and it can be used to look back in time, and to unlock secrets that can't be known any other way."

Caroline reached for the railing and slowly lowered her head. She could not see more than a few inches below the slight chop in the water. Her head was feeling heavy, but she was not dizzy. The boat began moving again, but at a slower speed.

Caroline thought about her family, her mother, Casey, even David, all isolated on this boat, this test tube in the bay. How her family had been brought together in Point Clear to resolve issues of the past. How Walker did the same by coming home to join his family. How Daniel came to hide out here, also with his family, to train as a prizefighter would, in this secret place of Point Clear. She had not talked to Daniel except for that one time after he left, and she felt their relationship dissolving. She wondered what would happen when she left Point Clear. Would she ever even see him again? Walker was really the only thing connecting them, and that could never be enough.

"I'd like to see the Everglades," Caroline said, not even thinking about the Everglades but remembering Casey as a two-year-old in a body cast. This was well before his jump off the house, the one that broke a bone in his foot so he had to walk around with a cane. This cast was from a jump off the couch that had broken his arm. "Do you think you'll be there awhile?"

Casey looked from the faraway water to Caroline. "I'm not sure, really," he said. "I'm just kind of living in the moment right now."

"That's cool," Caroline said. "Me too, actually." The cast had seemed so big, wrapping around his chest and enveloping his right arm, held out, ready, as if he were an usher at a wedding.

"You'd like the Everglades," he said.

"And you'd like New York."

"I can't believe I've never been."

"You should visit me while I'm still there." Caroline smiled at her brother, who was now looking away again. It was weird they were adults and he wasn't going to release a snake or a frog in her room or want to dress her up in football pads and box her. He slowly raised an arm to point.

There was a boat in the distance, a black police boat with a blue lightning stripe. Snorkelers were jumping overboard.

"They're looking for a body," Casey said.

Caroline watched the search team with intensity, not looking at anyone else. She stood up and walked toward her mother, who was already looking back at her with a knowing, sympathetic look. Caroline expected any second to see the men haul up Walker's dead body. She wondered why Walker would not leave a note, then began believing that he didn't want to make his departure so definite, as if leaving hope for his parents was kinder. Like how she didn't want to tell her mother about staying through the hurricane. In a strange way, Caroline still had hope that her father was alive. She had never seen his body. She had never seen a dead body. It still seemed like a faint possibility that her father could just one day appear.

Now the search crew was out of sight and Middle Bay Lighthouse was coming into view, the white hexagonal cottage with black shutters rising tall out of the water, towering above them on steel pilings and crisscrossing cables, with a red light perched on top—just as she'd seen in pictures on the Internet. It was amazingly intact; it had been built in 1885 yet had withstood every hurricane since. Seeing it up close after researching it, staring at pictures of it, then writing about it seemed very important to Caroline, seeing what Walker must have seen so many days in his life, and—if her imagination was right—on his last day.

David asked the captain about the green signs on the right and red signs on the left, and she explained they were channel markers. Then Casey asked about the depth of the channel, about the screw pilings the lighthouse was mounted on, and about the steel cables that connected them. Caroline thought about how uncertainties could wind around you, could cocoon you, blind you, increasing the tension, the stress, and weigh on you like something tangible. Maybe by facing the truth about herself and her past, the severity of her vertigo would be reduced. Maybe by taking her sabbatical here, she had cleared up direction, aiming for the Xs instead of the lines. Maybe all it would be from now on was a gradual reduction of stress and weight of confusion, and the vertigo would fade to nothing more than a nuisance she could live with, if it didn't vanish altogether.

She thought of Anderson Cooper and how he liked to go into dangerous places, to witness deep human suffering in order to report people's stories. Perhaps his need came from what happened to his brother. Like Anderson Cooper, she needed to bear witness—not to the truth about her own past, or not hers completely, but about Walker and their shared past.

Feeling she was not really herself anymore but Walker, and as the boat began to turn away from the lighthouse when she was not yet ready to leave it, she lifted herself up onto the railing, then pushed herself off of the boat and into the beautiful water. She closed her eyes and began to swim.

She was swimming underwater, and not until she began to feel the slight chill of it did she realize her hypnotic state. She rose to the surface and breathed, and without fear she began swimming to the steel cables, her head above the surface, only the Middle Bay Lighthouse in her vision, until she was climbing the cables, clinging to them. She stayed like that a moment, holding the steel in her hands, steel that somehow felt like magic in her hands, like life, like DNA.

Then, finally, she turned, fully herself again, and saw the boat circling back, with her family looking in shock at what she had done.

24. | Chapter One:
HOW IT ENDED

He stood at the waterline, letting the bay of his youth rock against his ankles, then stretched his arms behind his back until they bowed and loosened. He didn't want to think of the flecks of gray in his black hair, that he was thirty. Today he wanted to be fourteen.

He'd never had a brother or a sister and he remembered how intensely he'd wanted one, how he'd turned the water into one.

"Excuse me," he heard, faint words on the wind, so faint they might have been spoken to someone else, far away, but he looked around, doubting himself, and saw he wasn't alone. A blond woman stood on the beach behind him, someone he had never seen before, so he smiled, feeling caught, feeling fourteen.

"Doesn't the water look beautiful?" he said.

"It looks murky, but I suppose there's beauty in that," she said, and he liked that she shared his sense of the world. "Are you going to swim in it?" she asked.

She shared his sense of the world, so he relaxed. "Yes," he said. "Today's a good day for it."

He thought of telling her that he had swum after other hurricanes had passed, and tropical storms. He liked when there was even more salt water from the gulf mixed with the fresh water from rivers. She was quiet, and he liked that about her. She swept hair from her eyes and looked at him, then looked at the water. She, too, he thought, was drawn to the water.

He was happy for her. She hadn't evacuated either. She appeared about to cry.

Without thinking about what he was saying or even doing, he walked to her more than she did to him, and they introduced themselves, shaking hands, gently though, because her hand was as small in his as a blossom, while her eyes were red from sleeplessness.

As he spoke about where he lived, in his parents' guesthouse, he thought of how he'd left it moments ago. How he'd left the door unlocked as he always had. How he'd done noth-ing out of the ordinary except make his bed, because his mother would have liked that. It would've depressed him, discouraged him, to do anything else. Perhaps meeting Caroline and *identifying himself to her, he wondered, could be, for his parents' sake, his note.*

He could see that she liked to listen to people talk. So he kept talking. "My parents were already out of town, so I told them I'd get in the car and head north."

"My mom doesn't know either," she said.

"So we're both not supposed to be here," he said, and he wished she could have been with him at Stanford. He could have used someone on the swim team who understood him. Who would have hated the structure and rebelled against it with him. If she were only taller, more lan-guid, he thought. He could see, by her joints, she was comfortable with land. He hoped she could see that he was comfortable with water.

"I think I'm going back in and try to sleep," she said.

He nodded. "That's good," he said. "I'm going to do that soon myself."

"That's good," she said, nodding, too, and turned away. He watched her short stride, and then watched her turn toward him again. "It was nice to meet you," she said.

He tilted his head down, bent his knees, his body, until he was shaped like an S, so that he wasn't six foot six but five foot something and seeing her at eye level. "Maybe we'll meet each other again, Caroline," he told her. It was how his father would have spoken to her or to any-one else, always using names to ease people.

"I'd like to," she said, and he saw it had

worked. They had put each other at ease, even on a day like today, in the aftermath of a hurricane.

He unstuck his feet from the silky bog of mud and began to walk into the water. He was reminded of a million swim meets, all the crowded pools during warmup, how the water, though clearer, was almost this water, rocking, thrashing.

"Please, be careful," he heard Caroline say, but he didn't turn around. He kept walking, the water gradually rising higher along his legs. He was glad the hurricane had scattered the jellyfish elsewhere, that all he felt was water.

He was trying to focus, to block out the sky, all memories, all thoughts, all sounds. But he didn't want to be rude. He didn't want to trouble her. He wanted her to remain happy, as he was happy. Last night he'd decided, after going through all the boxes his parents had saved—a half dozen of them, of every medal and trophy and ribbon he'd ever won—that he'd swim only once more, that he'd swim in the bay. "I've swum in this bay a million times," he said, hoping that had sealed it. That they were now friends, trusted friends.

At waist-deep, he turned and lay leisurely back, and it was as if he had sandpapered his back the way he used to do his palms, because he felt the water eddy under him with great sensitivity. He'd never known the water this completely.

His arm strokes were slow, and his leg strokes weren't much faster. As he went farther and faced more turbulence, he knew he would have to adjust, reduce drag, increase rotation. Even so, at this pace, or close to this pace, he could backstroke six miles, to Middle Bay Lighthouse, easy. But today, pushing with his life, he thought he could swim twice that.

He relished that this was no warmup, this was no practice, there was no pace clock. No walls to interrupt his rhythm. He could stretch out his stroke and be the kid he was when he swam out into the bay for the first time. Or the kid he was later when he didn't stop, when he kept going until he reached Gaillard Island and sat on the beach laughing. Or the kid he was even later, at the age of twelve, when he didn't stop at Gaillard Island but kept going, dodging boats until he reached the opposite shore and, too tired to swim back, called a cab. Today, he was the totality of his youth, yet he was swimming farther into Mobile Bay than he thought, even then, that he ever would.

With his eyes closed, he imagined the map of Mobile Bay, which he had always seen as the relaxed foot of a swimmer. The heel at Bon Secour, the toes at Mobile, the arch at Point Clear. He imagined he could follow the channel past Gaillard Island and Middle Bay Lighthouse, that he could reach the ankle, the deepest waters. He imagined he could almost reach the gulf, and on today's faster current, he might.

Despite the arrhythmic movement of the bay, he was pinwheeling with ease and grace, and he decided to speed up his strokes. He'd been a happy child, and happy when he was swimming. He'd forgotten that sometimes, but he didn't forget that now, and he would never forget that again.

Then his left hand hit something it couldn't pass through, was stung and blocked simultaneously, and he was knocked out of rhythm. He opened his eyes to see what he'd struck—a floating section of pier decking, with rows of nails protruding along the planks. He checked his hand, and though it was bleeding from a puncture, it was a small wound. Nothing, he thought.

Once he'd swum around the decking, he closed his eyes, tried to forget the pain, and churned his arms and hips faster than before. He was forgetting the pain. That was why he was here today. To forget the medals he'd failed to win. To forget the Olympics and the Olympic trials. To forget college and computers and coming home, and that nothing ever satisfied him. Nothing but water and water alone.

He felt the water breaking ahead of him, so he opened his eyes, angled his head, and saw an overturned beacon. He dodged it. Then he dodged an ice chest, a submerged boat, a tree. According to the channel markers, he had swum three miles.

He loved his mother. He loved his father.

And they loved him. They wanted him to be happy. They wanted him to swim. They wanted him to love the water, and he did. It wasn't a matter of love.

He looked one last time at the sky, at streaks of gray clouds, at streaks of blue. He waited until a pelican passed overhead before he closed them again. He had always loved pelicans, their low glide over water that he had tried to emulate in water, their courageous plunge down into it that he hoped to emulate. Then he told himself not to open his eyes again. Regardless of what happened, regardless of what he touched or what touched him. He had made mistakes with his eyes, looking around before the finish. His eyes had failed him. His body never had.

But his body wasn't perfect. He started to feel soreness and exhaustion coming. But he didn't slow. He was calm and steady and fast. He knew he had more miles in him. This was the best part, the last part, the struggle, the well-fought finish. Waiting to die any other way would have been tragic.

He knew that if he opened his eyes and turned his head he would see Middle Bay Lighthouse rising out of the water on steel pilings laced with cables. If he were a boy, he'd want to race to it and cling to the cables. He'd want to climb them, as if he were climbing the limbs of a tree, like the limbs of the live oak in the yard at home, and when he had reached the deck and flung himself over the railing, maybe he would have found the windows broken from the hurricane, this clapboard cottage almost a replica of his home—unlocked, and white with black shutters.

But he felt like a boy still, racing past Middle Bay Lighthouse for the greater challenge. In the gulf, his body wouldn't be searched for and wouldn't be found. He didn't want his body to be found. The body of a swimmer should not be buried in the ground.

25. | THE TREE SWING

After returning from Middle Bay Lighthouse, her clothes and hair still wet, her family still shocked, Caroline had said good-bye, retreated to her room, and had written in a rush. Then with her chapter revised, she had showered and dressed in her tennis clothes, and now was sitting on the bed flipping channels.

The last Caroline had heard was that Ivan had vanished somewhere over Texas. She wondered if he had become integrated with other lows, other highs, and had since become a mist over somewhere needing mist. She didn't know. He could be anywhere. Apparently, like Ivan, like everyone eventually, Walker had made his impact and vanished.

Since Walker's disappearance, she had tuned in to the local news whenever she could, when she'd thought of it. If there had been any update on Walker, she had missed it. She decided she couldn't wait any longer. If she wanted news, she'd have to call for it.

A female dispatcher answered, and Caroline believed, wanted to believe, it was the same one she'd met, with orange-brown hair and stooped shoulders, who'd held out her hands as if they were buckets catching rain.

"Detective Bowers, please," Caroline said.

"Sure, he's right here, hold on," the woman said.

Caroline stretched the cord to the French doors and watched a yacht with ST. CROIX across its bow in brass letters sail into the harbor. Then she heard a click on the line.

"Detective Bowers," he answered.

"Yes, hi, Detective Bowers," she said, "this is Caroline Berry. The one you spoke to about Walker Galloway."

"Right, right," he said. "How can I help you?"

"Well," she said, "I'm sorry to call like this. I know you're busy."

"That's all right. Whatcha need?"

"I'm going back home tomorrow," she said, "so I was wondering if there was any news about him, anything you can share."

She heard the creak of his chair. "I'm sorry," he said. "I wish I could tell you something, and I would, but we don't have anything. The last word on this came from you, actually."

"Oh, okay," she said, feeling a sense of relief, which didn't surprise her. "I just had to know."

"That's all right. You can call any time. It's no bother."

"Okay, good, I may do that," she said, but as soon as she heard herself say that, she knew she wouldn't call again.

After she hung up, she put on her tennis shoes. It was time for her last lesson with Joseph.

As usual, he was already on the court waiting and prepared with his racquet and a shopping cart of balls. He didn't have his sword, but he was wearing a green baseball cap with a detailed colored design on it. When he saw her, he opened his arms wide, not to hug her but as a grand marshal would lead a parade.

"'I will arise and go now, and go to Innisfree,' " he said, and he continued until he'd recited the entire poem, one by Yeats that Caroline recognized, remembering a teacher reciting it in class, though not this well, this theatrically, this Irish.

She laughed and clapped. She didn't know what to say. She felt emotional making this day a day of goodbyes.

"I hope you continue with your writing," he said. He looked at her with his head lowered.

She still wasn't sure what the tattoolike design was. She could tell it was a woman, though not a fairy. Maybe a mermaid.

"Listen to me," he said. "You'll have to disappear into your room months at a time and churn out words. It'll be like a word factory inside your head. It's the same thing with tennis. You have to go into your own world. People just don't get it. They'll think you're a weirdo, but you're like a really social girl, but you have to have your mind so clear, and it's a state of mind—almost like having a Holy Communion with yourself on a daily basis."

The Virgin Mary, that's what was on his hat.

"I just view writing as like something that's a sacred gift, like if you have the ability to take words out of your head and make them flow like a river in a book and people love to read it, then that's what life is about." He smiled. "One of the things that life is about."

In her final lesson, she was in her own world, she was in the moment, she was visualizing, and she learned the buggy whip.

She hit the shot again and again, her racquet flying over her head.

"Oh, yeah, Caroline. That's it. Beautiful. You got it!"

After the lesson, she was stronger and was able to say good-bye without her voice breaking, or coming close to that.

"Go forth and buggy whip," he said and slapped her hand in what felt to Caroline like slow motion.

"Thank you," she said, and he nodded.

From the courts, she walked to the golf shop, where she rented a golf cart to tour the courses. The Azalea course was closed due to too many downed trees, but Dogwood was open, so off she went, following the paths her grandfather had followed, and her father had followed. The paths crisscrossed, and she was afraid she'd get lost, then was afraid that she *was* lost, and became certain of it when she started passing what looked like freight cars filled with dead trees resting on fairways. But when she found a lake with an island green, the fourteenth hole of the Azalea course, she didn't care and stopped her cart. It was almost an island, really a tree-shaped peninsula, with the lake nearly encircling it in the shape of a *C.* She thought of her father and the disconnected *C* on the Cheever book. She thought of her name. She'd been conceived here, she thought, probably conceived here. She knew she'd been conceived here.

She got back behind the tiny black wheel and continued along paths until she'd found Confederate Rest Cemetery. She stopped, though this time she didn't get out. From the cart, she could see the wooden crosses of the nameless dead, could see the wrought-iron bench beneath the cedars. She turned and gazed at the trees that had once held the sun at sunset. She closed her eyes, imagining a kiss on her forehead, on her lips, on her neck. Then she opened her eyes, and sighed, and drove on, stopping only once more at the driving range.

After she returned the golf cart, she walked back to her room and checked her messages, but she didn't have any. So she took a quick shower and changed into her swimsuit, though not to backstroke this time. To swim her own stroke, her brief, sputtering underwater stroke, her signature.

She swam in each pool and sat briefly in each hot tub, then wrapped a towel about her waist, ordered a chicken wrap and fries, and ate her dinner watching her last sunset. Her last pelicans, soaring. Her last pelicans, diving. Her last seagulls, crying and fighting for the fries that she'd left unguarded.

Once the sun began to set into the bay, she left her deck chair to walk out to the beach where other hotel guests were gathered, and the setting came fast—in seconds. Then, as soon as the sun vanished, everyone scattered. They went back to their rooms, their deck chairs. Caroline strolled the beach alone.

The gate of the picket fence at the third house still stood open, as if it had been designed against closure. As if a permanent welcome were in order there. So Caroline walked through. She walked through the deep blue air, across the wide lawn, and began to reach out her arms before she found them, and then she found them, the coarse twisted cords of the tree swing, and sat down on the plank seat.

The only room in the house that appeared lit was the kitchen. Caroline could see through the walls, see the rooms, see Mrs. Galloway losing her balance and spinning until she'd passed out on the floor in front of the kitchen sink. She could see Mrs. Galloway holding herself, as if to prop herself up to keep from falling again. She could feel Mrs. Galloway's arms like these hard, dead ropes. Then a ghost of movement swept past the windows of the kitchen door, and she could see Mr. Galloway pacing. She thought this time she could see this. And when she saw nothing else, only the stillness of light, she could see Mr. Galloway deciding to sit at the table to finish his coffee.

She could see Mr. Galloway checking his watch, soon after dark, thinking, *Any minute now.*

Caroline thought of her own father. How he'd been devoted to his family, but also to Phillips Petroleum. He'd been in charge of all marketing activities in Oklahoma, Arkansas, and Louisiana, supervising over a thousand service stations. But working at Phillips was like working for Xerox or any big company. There could be lay-offs. She thought of what her father had said to her not long after being forced into retirement: "One day your life is great, and the next day you wake up and there is no place to go."

She pressed her heels against the ground, then lifted them to let herself swing.

26. | A CHANGING ENVIRONMENT

Before she slept her last night in the Grand Hotel and left Point Clear, she was compelled to open her laptop once more and consider an alternate ending to her last version. Her brother might someday read her book, so she wanted the science to be true, since it is in our DNA to adapt, to need to live, to want to live. Between accident and intent, it was the logical compromise.

He knew that if he opened his eyes and turned his head he would see Middle Bay Lighthouse rising out of the water on steel pilings laced with cables. If he were a boy, he'd want to race to it and cling to the cables. He'd want to climb them, as if he were climbing the limbs of a tree, like the limbs of the live oak in the yard at home, and when he had reached the deck and flung himself over the railing, maybe he would have found the windows broken from the hurricane, this clapboard house almost a replica of the guesthouse—unlocked, and white with black shutters.

It depressed him that he didn't want to do what he would have done, if he were a boy. True, in the gulf, his body wouldn't be searched for and wouldn't be found. He didn't want his body to be found. The body of a swimmer should not be buried in the ground. But maybe, he hesitated to tell himself, he could live to swim again. Maybe to swim from here to the gulf next time, tomorrow if not tonight. After a nap first in the lighthouse. Maybe he should consider this race in legs.

He knew this was nothing more than the convincing delirium of fear talking. Struggle, he told himself. Struggle.

He fought to churn his arms and shoulders. His legs now barely kicked. You fought well, he told himself. You fought well.

He'd swum about as far as he could, about as far as he'd expected. The natural flow of the water would sweep him the rest of the way, through the pass between Fort Gaines and Fort Morgan, to the Gulf of Mexico. He would just need one last push.

It was what he would do if he were a

boy. To imagine a line of rainbow-colored flags passing like birds overhead to indicate the approaching finish, the approaching wall, and then the look of surprise in the stands when he didn't stop, didn't hold up his arms in victory, but kept going—rolling over, flipping, then pushing from the wall to glide into a dolphin kick and begin again.

He began to count. And by his massive stretch and pull and the last-gasp damming of his hands, he knew the count would be to three.

And when he reached three, his recovery arm crossed his face as his face turned to the water, then he rolled over onto his stomach, tucking his arms in, and he flipped elegantly.

He wished he had an audience to see it. He wished his parents could see him. He remembered how that felt. That was why he swam, in the beginning. To awe them with what for him, not for them, was easy. Then, as he completed the turn, thrusting his legs as if he were pushing off a wall, he sucked the water, the cool taste of salt, into his lungs. But he stalled. Because there was no wall to push off from. So he stopped moving. He stopped swimming. He stopped imagining, and his eyes opened— to the brackish water his vision could not penetrate—and he realized his mistake.

PART
FIVE

27. CITY FLOWERS

This was the first time Caroline had ever knocked on her own door. "Emma?" she said. "Are you there?" She opened the door slowly, then peered in. She walked through the entryway, then into the small kitchen, where she checked her voice mail. There were no messages.

She walked into the living room and set her bags down by the couch. The place was empty. And very clean. There was a stack of mail on the coffee table, which Caroline quickly glanced through, and then she noticed the note.

> *Dear Caroline,*
> *Thank you very much for letting me stay here. I loved it! You'll notice the place is very clean. I wanted to show my appreciation and clean the place, but I'm no good at that, so I called a maid service. I think they did an excellent job! Call me when you get settled.*
>
> *Love,*
> *Emma*

*P.S. Here is the mail—just a few bills and catalogues.
Also, a friend of yours from high school called—Sally—she
was very nice. She said call whenever you want, nothing
important. She just wanted to catch up. Also, a woman
(I'm sorry I can't remember her name, Kathy maybe?—I
didn't write it down) called about playing doubles at the
UN. I didn't know they had a tennis court there! You don't
need to call her, she said. She'll call you to play another
time. That's it. Thank you again!*

Caroline walked through an arched door to her bedroom,
which was so small it could only fit a full-size bed and a very
small dresser. Caroline loved the room, though. She thought it
was romantic with the radiator, and with the window where
you could partially view Union Square Park.

She leaned over and opened the window. You could lie on
the bed backwards and look out the window, and that was what
she was doing, feeling a cool breeze and listening to New York.
She thought about her first few weeks in the city, how she'd kept
a journal, and later, when she looked back on it, smiled at how
in love she was with everything. Everything—the noise, the
trash, the smell of sewage, homeless people, prostitutes, the
political activists, and, of course, all the fashionable-looking
NYU kids, all the tattoos, the earrings everywhere, wearing a
dress over jeans, or having streaks of any color in their hair. She
remembered the first time she walked into the Tisch School of
the Arts and took a screenwriting class and met Emma. It was
thrilling for her to go into that building. They had posters on the
walls of movies from former students, Spike Lee, Martin
Scorsese, Oliver Stone, and it seemed then that anything was
possible.

Caroline walked to her closet. She put on jeans and boots

and a small black sweater that just hit her waist. It was fall in New York, so she could wear her black leather jacket. She wanted to walk around Union Square. It was beginning to get dark, and soon the place would be a crisscrossing maze of people.

Outside, she glanced up and down Fifteenth Street—there were two bars, two restaurants, a grocery store, a dry cleaner, an off-Broadway theater, Irving Plaza, where they had live music (one time she had seen Julian Casablancas standing out front, waiting for someone, she supposed, his brown eyes seeing her, then looking upward). On her street she had seen Ethan Hawke, Tim Robbins, Ric Ocasek, Hillary Clinton, and Julia Roberts. She felt she could see just about anyone there.

She began walking to Union Square Park, hoping for a celebrity sighting but not seeing anyone. Crossing the street, it occurred to her that it didn't matter. She was back in New York with the incense tables, the skateboarders, the guy with the IMPEACH CHENEY sign. These were her people, and she was honored to walk among them.

She didn't know how long she would stay in New York—not forever, she guessed, but awhile longer. She was only twenty-seven, and she would find a job somewhere. Maybe a temp job, where she could leave any time and not feel any guilt. Finishing her novel was all that mattered. She owed that to Walker, her father, herself, to tell their story. She could work at a bank or a law office. It didn't matter. She had heard of actors and writers working odd hours—the all-night shift, weekends—and making good money, and she could do that, too.

She walked through the park and all the way to Sixth Avenue, to Gray's Papaya, where she got the Recession Special, two hot dogs and an orange drink for $2.50. A man next to her was drooling, and that was okay, and another man said something about elastic, and Caroline ignored him and stared out the window, eating and drinking, watching people go by.

It began to get a bit cooler as she was walking back, and rowdier. Saturday night was approaching, and there was an excitement in the air—packs of young guys swaggering, girls walking in those heels that always made Caroline amazed that they could do it.

She began thinking of Point Clear and the heels she wore on her first date with Daniel. She thought of the small steps she had to take when walking on the sidewalk in Fairhope. Then she thought of flowers. *You really loved flowers as a little girl. The city has its own horticulturalist, used to be the mayor. The blooms from the crepe myrtle were wilted in Walker's yard. The single yellow flower in the slender vase was a mum.* She thought of flowers, and she felt she had to have some.

She walked to the deli on Park and Nineteenth with all the flowers out front. She picked an assortment of colors—pink, red, yellow, purple, blue, white. What were they? Carnations? Posies? Lilies? She wasn't sure—she would learn, though. She was learning all the time. Snapdragons? Lilacs? Orchids? Daisies? She would do the research. She would find out. She took them all to the counter and paid, and then she watched a man who did not seem to speak English wrap them in colorful spiral funnels of pastel tissue paper. Then he motioned for her to cradle her arms the way he was doing, so she did, and he stacked into her arms all seven bundles.

Spiraling with flowers, she walked down the street. She could hardly see in front of her, but in her periphery she could see the quick walk of New Yorkers, walking ghosts, going by so fast, or was her vision blurring? She had to keep her head still and straight, keep walking down Park until Fifteenth, then make a left, three more blocks. Streamers of light from oncoming traffic and stoplights, green and yellow and red, those walking ghosts next to her who weren't real, just her vision blurring, her vertigo. A hallucination of motion, yet real motion, too. She had to concentrate.

She kept walking—Seventeenth, Sixteenth—getting closer to her street, the ghosts becoming Walker, with his dark V-shaped hair and intense eyes, then her father, with his sloping shoulders and narrow blue eyes. Then, turning onto Fifteenth, she saw a vertical box of red in front of her: Walker, her father, Walker, her father, solid red, something real, something she could touch it was so real.

He was standing in front of her building, waiting for her, wearing his thin, long-sleeved red shirt.

She walked to him and lowered the bundles of flowers still in her arms, and he took them from her and carefully laid them down between them.

She could hardly believe he was there. She looked down to his black shorts that blended into the night, but his legs were tan and seemed to glow, and his white tennis shoes were so white, and his racquet bag on the sidewalk was enormous, blue and black, and then there was another bag, a black duffel bag.

Daniel was looking at her, too, she thought, as if he knew her completely, though they did not speak, not yet. Time was not real here. She was somewhere else, someone else. She was her father about to kiss her mother in the garden, with all those flowers at their feet.

"Walker," he said, and she was brought back and nodded. "Walker," he said again, but from how he said the name, she did not know what he would say next.

28. | LAST CHAPTER

He'd needed to relax, untangle himself, and decide what his next step in life should be, and for once, he thought, he'd accomplished precisely what he'd wanted. With nothing left to eat or drink or use or wear, it was now time, and he was ready to go home.

He didn't want to leave the place a mess, but since there wasn't a way for him to dispose of his trash, he stuffed as much of it as he could—empty cans of tuna fish, baked beans, Vienna Sausages, the empty water, Coke, and Gatorade bottles, candy wrappers, spent matches, dead batteries—in the ice chests he'd brought, then stacked what remained neatly on top of them. Then he folded his blanket and laid it at the base of the spiral staircase leading to the light. And on the blanket he put his radio, his kerosene lamp, a blue ballpoint pen, and a spiral notebook, which he'd written in each day, recording his activities—swimming, eating—observations about birds and fish and tides, memories, random thoughts, and notes in pseudo code

```
0 = cylindrical spiral. >0 = conical (fixable to phi/fibonacci)
Variable rotation rates both clockwise and counter clockwise
{
x = g * t * cos((t + offset + rot) % 360)
y = g * t * sin((t + offset + rot) % 360)
z = g * d * t
Transform3DLocalToWorldCoords()
DisplayPoint()
}
```

for a computer program on spirals, which were everywhere, in hurricanes, galaxies, chromosomes, a seashell, this staircase, this notebook. He would come back to clean up. He would come back for the notebook.

He eased the door open and peeked out, seeing a couple of boats in the far distance but nothing nearby, except for a sleeping pelican perched on the railing of the balcony a few feet away. When he opened the door wider and its hinges creaked, the pelican startled and burst into flight, and Walker felt the wind from its wings as he stepped out to shut the door behind him.

He checked the door to make sure that it

stayed shut, that he'd repaired the damage he'd done when he forced it open. How long ago that was he didn't exactly know, weeks, he supposed. It was the day of the hurricane, just after it had passed, when it was still dark, before day-break. When of course it was risky to take his father's boat out, with all the wreckage in the bay, but the hurricane had inspired him. He'd returned home to Point Clear, thinking that with no place else to go he might die there, thinking more and more he might die there, that he might as well die there, but riding out the hurricane had inspired him not to quit again but to rise up with a new beginning, at least to try. If he only had another place where he could duplicate the hurricane and hide out for longer and save himself, until he wasn't merely inspired but whole again, completely new. And then it came to him, thinking of the bay of his youth, where he had gone before when he had hoped to reach something almost unreachable— that is, if the hurricane hadn't destroyed it.

As he climbed onto the railing of the bal-cony and stood where the pelican had slept, he smiled, remembering the moment of his decision and the calm, deliberate passion that followed. How he'd stocked his father's boat with every-thing he thought he'd need, plus a crowbar to force the door open, and he carefully made his way here. Then once he'd unloaded the supplies inside the lighthouse, using a rope as a pul-ley, he returned the boat, since it was his father's boat, and since a boat tethered to a piling below would have given away where he was, or where someone was, hiding out in a historic landmark out of commission, and he swam back, following the safe route he'd found by boat, which was the same route he was about to take again, again just as the sun was rising, though this time, instead of swimming the backstroke alone, he'd swim the medley.

He felt taller than six-six here on the railing of Middle Bay Lighthouse. Even as he sprung forward into a dive and split the surface of the bay. Even as he began to dolphin kick and glide upward toward the light and row his arms into the butterfly, he felt taller.

He thought of the blond girl he'd seen on the beach after the hurricane, how she was the last person he'd spoken to and touched, her hand as small in his as a blossom, and how he'd heard a motor and peeked through a window and seen her (Was it days later? Weeks later? He didn't know) like an apparition, diving for him, it seemed, from a chartered boat. He remembered how he'd stayed still inside until he'd heard the boat turn away, and he peeked out again and saw her on board, wrapped with a towel, her hair darkened by water. He remembered thinking when he first met her that she was drawn to the water, that they could have been friends, that she seemed like him, and he'd been right. He remembered how good that had made him feel to be right.

Gaillard Island was coming into view when he sensed in his muscles and in the currents that it was time to begin the second leg of his medley, so he straightened his arms and extended them, as if to touch a wall, then rolled over and began pinwheeling his arms in the backstroke.

When he passed the island and his right hand put in, he rolled over and began the breaststroke. He was thirsty, but he was calm. He felt light and new and strong, as if something recently born of water, but he had to acknowledge he was thirsty. That he would never get enough of water.

His parents would be happy to see him, but he thought they'd be happier to see that he, too, was happy to see them. He'd disappeared before and had come back without a change. He thought they deserved this change in him more than he did. He hoped he hadn't worried them any.

Occasionally, he saw a mullet jump ahead of him, then a seagull or pelican dive after it, but mostly, above water or below water, he saw water, sometimes appearing blue or green, depending on the underwater topography or the angle of the sun breaking through the clouds.

As he began the last leg of freestyle, he felt his body slowing, almost plunging. He was hungry, too. Hungry for food and hungry for land, to breathe again on land. He could feel it in his legs and his arms, but mostly in his lungs. He wasn't simply thirsty.

He'd been rationing his food and water to survival levels for the last few days. He didn't want to leave too soon. He didn't want to feel like he was quitting.

As he swam past the last beacon, he knew if he lifted his head above the water he would see pier pilings rising up in staggered formations along the eastern shore. He wouldn't see his house, the guesthouse, or his parents' house, but he would see the trees and the picket fence.

He finally had to fight himself to churn his arms and shoulders and kick his legs, even to rotate his head to breathe. He could see the muddy bottom beneath him now, slowly rising up to meet him. He was almost there.

And then he was there, where he could swim no more and was kneeling in the mud and gasping, blinking his eyes at the white houses with black shutters.

He leaned forward and the ground melted away, filling his fists with mud, so he crawled forward until the ground felt a little firmer, with sand with the silt, and he tried again to stand. Though he wobbled, with his hands and feet sinking some, he managed to rise up and stay up, and he began to walk, his clumsy, fatigued body nearly collapsing at the joints at each step, across the beach, then through the open gate into his parents' yard.

He passed the guesthouse, but then he turned back to the guesthouse and felt for the key above the door. It was there. He was glad. He *was worried he'd forgotten to lock up and leave it where they always left it.*

When he reached the back door to his parents' house, he was hardly able to stop himself from continuing forward and nearly fell into the door, but he caught himself, then righted himself, and took a deep breath before he knocked. He didn't remember ever having knocked on his parents' door.

It seemed he was waiting a long time to see someone appear in the window, and then Walker saw his father's shadow slanting across the wall, if not racing, with curious speed.

A bluish light filtered through the blinds, and Caroline began to hear the sounds of New York before the morning rush—the wailing brakes of garbage trucks, the clanking raising of metal storefronts. Daniel was asleep in her bed. At that moment, he wasn't winning and he wasn't losing. His best friend was alive, and he'd come to see her and to tell her the news, and now he was simply asleep.

She'd been writing for hours the truth about Walker. Daniel had been angry at times when telling her what had happened. But she wasn't angry. She looked forward to meeting him again one day. She felt she should thank him.

She closed her laptop, then her eyes, and imagined herself on the beach that morning after the hurricane. She imagined herself walking into the water, swimming her stroke in the water's beautiful patterned confusion, then spinning under, tasting salt, and being pulled to air by a man she didn't know, a tall, languid man who was a swimmer, simply going swimming after a storm, a man who was saving her.

ACKNOWLEDGMENTS

Many people helped me with many subjects as I was writing this book. I'm especially grateful to my wonderful friend Lauren Rosolen (film and Emma), Pete Davis (computer programming), Jon Isaacson (vertigo), Lem Hagler and Ray Flumerfelt (Tulsa and the oil industry), David X Williams (science and Casey), Julia and A. N. Hall (David), and Joseph O'Dwyer (tennis, Ireland, and the Seagull). Sena Maddison's article in *Social Occasions* alerted me to the world-class tennis being played at the Point Clear Tennis and Swim Club (and led me to the excellent teacher Joseph O'Dwyer). *Gold in the Water* by P. H. Mullen was an invaluable source and great inspiration. The Grand Hotel is a real and beautiful place in Point Clear, though certainly used fictitiously for the plot of the novel. Many thanks to Will St. Paul, whose parents honeymooned at the Grand Hotel, Sonny Brewer for the big idea, and Becky and Tom Hemphill for the ride to Middle Bay Lighthouse. Also, thanks to Charlotte Cabaniss Robertson, Martin Lanaux, Jim Gilbert, Doug Kelley, Carol Mason, Tom Jenks, and my wise agent, Michelle Tessler. Thanks to my talented editor and friend, Amanda Patten, my terrific publicist, Kimberly Brissenden, and to the rest of the Touchstone publishing team: Mark Gompertz, Trish Todd, Chris Lloreda, Betsy Haglage, Tricia Wygal, Heather McNallie, Marie Florio, Patti Ratchford, and the many others there who helped this book along.

I'm also grateful to what feels like everyone in my hometown of Fort Smith and by extension the state of Arkansas (with special thanks to Jane Thompson at the Arkansas State Library, Amy Jordan and Jennifer Goodson at the Fort Smith Public Library, Cynthia Echternach, and the Walkers) for support of *A Secret Word*. Also, thanks to Brady and Christy Paddock, Jane Daines, and my old friends from D.C. (especially Stacey Sturner and Tom Walls), and good friends Tory Dee, Sally, and Ann. Thanks to Alice and Amber. Thanks to Mary Ann McCarty. Thanks to my cousin Marianne, my first family member (besides my mother) to read *A Secret Word*, Josh Jackson and David Shuman (whom I should have already thanked), Patti Collins and the Thompsons, and Maggie and Lemuria—I'll never forget my first reading there.

And, of course, much love and thanks to my mother, Anita Paddock, and to my husband, Sidney Thompson.

Point Clear

Summary

Twenty-seven-year-old Caroline Berry is living a
life of drifting solitude in New York City, working two
jobs while her dream of being a writer is slowly fading.
Unfulfilled, a little lost, and suffering from an intensify-
ing case of vertigo, she makes an uncharacteristically
bold decision to leave her jobs in an attempt to jump-
start her life and writing career, which leads her to a
retreat at a grand old southern hotel—a favorite of her
late grandfather's—in Point Clear, Alabama.

No sooner does she arrive than Hurricane Ivan
strikes, and instead of evacuating with the other hotel
guests, Caroline secretly cloisters herself there until it
passes. When a man she chances to meet on the beach
in the storm's aftermath ends up missing, Caroline

can't help being drawn into his life as she tries to sort out her own.

Discussion Points

1. Caroline's vertigo first manifests after she learns about her grandfather's death. How does its development highlight and symbolize the dizzying disconnection she feels to everything around her?

2. Caroline believes that "the death of someone you loved would always color everything," and that you can never get over it. How do the deaths of her father and grandfather color her life?

3. Compare Caroline's almost suicidal desire to risk the storm from her hotel room and her imagined versions of Walker's post-storm swim in the bay. Do you think Caroline really wanted to die in the hurricane? Did you think that Walker really wanted to die in the bay?

4. Caroline remembers her family as "close" during their years surviving tornadoes in Tulsa, and feels that her time in the hurricane is just as important, even though she is alone. Why does she feel this way?

5. When Anderson Cooper comes to the hotel to cover the approach of Hurricane Ivan, Caroline muses that there is a kind of connection through grief between herself (due to her father's car accident) and Anderson Cooper and his mother (due to the tragic death of his brother/her son). Do you agree with this theory?

6. Why do you think the author chose to create Walker and Daniel—best friends—as highly accomplished, professional athletes who haven't quite attained the pinnacle of their careers? How does this compare with Caroline's abandonment of tennis after her father's death, or her avoidance of writing a novel while living in New York City?

7. Caroline mentions several times that she feels like she and Walker are "the same person." What similarities are there? Why is this connection important to the development of the novel?

8. In the final lines of *Point Clear,* Caroline implies that Walker "saved" her. How has her obsession with Walker and her deliberate forays into his life revitalized her own?

9. Discuss the significance of the title *Point Clear,* to the characters and to the overall meaning of the novel.

10. If you've read Jennifer Paddock's first novel, *A Secret Word,* how do you think *Point Clear* compares? Do you see similarities of style, character development, or voice? How do you think Paddock is developing as a writer?

Enhance Your Book Club Experience

1. Take some time to do a little research on competitive sports, such as tennis and swimming, so you can get inside Caroline, Daniel, and Walker's world. Report your impressions to your book club and discuss how your newly acquired information has or hasn't changed your perspective on the characters.

2. Get some ideas about what it's like to live in Alabama—its history, beaches, festivals, and landmarks—by visiting tourist websites to give yourself a point of reference.

Author Q&A

1. What made you choose the opening epigraph from John Cheever for this novel?

It captures every important aspect of the novel—the lush botanical setting of Point Clear; the hope and struggle of each character to develop into a better, more enlightened person; and the tendency people in general have, like plants, to gravitate toward a physical embodiment of light, whether that light is the noon sun, a setting sun, an elegant lighthouse, or the lights of New York City.

2. Caroline comes from Tulsa and moves to New York City to study creative writing at NYU—a very similar background to yours, given that you moved from Arkansas to New York City and also studied creative writing at NYU.

What other similarities are there between you and your heroine?

Caroline and I are not the healthiest of eaters or drinkers (I drink about three cans of Coke a day), but I'm trying to do better. We both love tennis and see it as an art form. We both swim best under water. We both lost our fathers in a sudden way and have an interest in our family's history. We both suffer from vertigo, though Caroline's is much more severe (my mother has had episodes of vertigo almost exactly like Caroline's). And although I'm not from Tulsa, I did live there for one year, going to school and playing on the tennis team at the University of Tulsa.

3. You spent several years working in book publishing. Do you think this benefited you as a published author?

A prominent writer once told me not to work in publishing, that it would in no way be helpful to me as a writer, that it would strip the romance and depress me. But I do like that I understand the process of how a manuscript makes it into print and know what an honor it is to be published. It seems a bit of a miracle, when you see just how many people can say no along the way.

4. This is your second novel. How was the experience different from writing your first?

For my first novel, even though there are three main characters, I was mostly writing about myself, as if I had divided myself into three parts, so that even the most imagined scenes and characters were inspired by very similar actual ones. For this novel, however, I committed myself to doing a lot of research on a number of subjects, such as swimming and hurricanes. I even spent a lot of time learning about the latest trends and techniques in the tennis world, a subject I thought I already knew quite a lot about.

5. Caroline's desire to ride out the storm alone in the hotel seems like an adult version of the common childhood dream of camping out in a museum or shopping mall surreptitiously. Have you ever indulged in such a fantasy?

No, I haven't, but I've always liked the idea of being somewhere I'm not supposed to be. I remember in high school sneaking out in the middle of the night with friends and just driving around—not doing anything wrong or illegal, but by just being out and not asleep in our beds, we were thrilled.

6. Have you ever experienced an intense storm like the tornadoes and hurricanes described in Point Clear*?*

I remember tornadoes in Arkansas, one in particular that happened in the middle of the night when I was staying at my grandparents' house, and we had to go outside to the dark storm cellar for shelter, our only light being a flashlight, which was exciting for me. When we emerged from the cellar after the storm, you couldn't even see the house. All of the huge pecan trees had been uprooted and had fallen all around it, but none onto it, and we felt really lucky. I live now in Point Clear, Alabama, and although I did not stay through Ivan or Katrina, I was here for the preparations— boarding windows, buying supplies. There is a reckless, joyous excitement before each storm—a defiant "we are all in this together" spirit—until the storm arrives, of course, and there is real devastation.

7. You live in Fairhope, Alabama—a town that makes an appearance in Point Clear. *Are there other stories brewing in your head about your current home region?*

I actually live in Point Clear, which is right next to Fairhope, where I've lived as well. By writing this book and learning the history of the Grand Hotel, Confederate Rest Cemetery, and Middle Bay Lighthouse, my attachment to the area has grown stronger, far beyond the mere fact of its obvious beauty. I do think I'll write more about this area, and more about Arkansas, and more about New York. I'm hoping to write a third book that would connect *A Secret Word,* my first book, and *Point Clear,* making a trilogy. I always like it when writers connect their books when their books beg to be connected.

8. You leave the reader completely unsure of Walker's status until the very end of the novel. Were you in as much suspense as your readers?

In my first draft of the novel, the story was about a swimmer who walks into the water after a hurricane with the clear intention of dying. Then a writer friend, Sonny Brewer, had the idea that my character could swim instead to Middle Bay Lighthouse, making a spiritual quest of sorts to match Caroline's. I thought the idea seemed crazy, but the more I learned about swimming, how strong swimmers could be, especially in open water, I found it could be possible. But the swimmer would have to be an elite swimmer, which Walker is.

9. Caroline seeks to sort out her life by writing about it, partly through the eyes of her imagined version of Walker. Have you used your writing to sort out moments in your own life, and if so, how?

My work, as a whole, is often autobiographical. Writing about your life, it seems to me, is a way of participating in it, getting closer to it, examining it, realizing what might have happened or how what happened might have changed you.

10. This novel is very complex: a love story, a strange developing illness, a (late) coming-of-age family drama, grief of all kinds, a mysterious disappearance, and a writer in process. What kind of experience do you most want your readers to enjoy when reading Point Clear?

The experience each reader needs most. Hopefully, it can provide that.

Turn the page for a look at
JENNIFER PADDOCK'S
incandescent debut novel—

a luminous story of friendship and family, sex
and secrets, growing up and growing apart.

0-7432-4707-8

Available wherever books are sold or at www.simonsays.com.

TOUCHSTONE
A Division of Simon & Schuster
A CBS COMPANY

The Ones Who Are
Holding Things Up

November 1986

Chandler

Leigh is the kind of girl who hangs around girls who get in fights. Not that she wears rock-concert T-shirts, but she does smoke. She and I are different, but we are friends. She's been to my house, three stories with woods and a lake in back, a game room, halls you can do cartwheels down. And I've been to her house, dark and small and sad.

Sarah is beautiful and theatrical and is my best friend and has been since the day I almost killed her. When we were eight, she talked the assistant golf pro into letting us hit range balls, and she walked right behind me on my backswing. There was screaming and blood and an ambulance, and seventeen stitches to the back of her head in the shape of a *C,* my own initial.

Then we began taking tennis lessons and now are known as *those tennis girls*. A tournament can get us out of school for a week. We go to a public school and make good grades without studying. We are on the outside of the inner circle of cool kids but are cool enough.

I'm in Spanish class zoning out, not listening to the scratchy record of a Mexican family having a conversation at breakfast. I'm thinking about my plan for lunch today with Leigh and Sarah, maybe at the country club, and wondering how that would go.

My father tells me that where we live, in Fort Smith, Arkansas, used to be called "Hell on the Border." It was a place people passed through: Cherokee Indians on the Trail of Tears, gold miners to California, trappers canoeing upriver, ranchers headed to Texas, outlaws seeking freedom.

I imagine there are worse places to grow up, and I am lucky to be rich and to love my parents, but I do not love it here. I will pass through.

Between first and second period, at my locker, I see Leigh at her locker, tapping a pack of Camel Lights, and when she catches my eye, I start to walk over, but somebody, a real genius of slapstick, comes up behind me and pushes the back side of my right knee, causing my leg to buckle, and I almost trip. I turn around with a little agitation and find Sarah smiling her coy Sarah smile.

"Falling apart at the seams, Chandler?" she says. Then Trey, the running back, rushes Sarah, taking her in a headlock, holding her like he's in love, and I wonder if Sarah notices this, and when he lets go, there is purple dye smeared across his white jersey. Sarah is always dying her hair. She probably just did it thirty minutes ago, staying home during first period, using one of the drawerful of late notes her mom has written for her.

I watch Trey pushing Sarah down the hall.

"Trey's walking me to class," Sarah yells back. "I'll meet you on the court."

Second period Sarah and I have gym, and so does Leigh, but Coach McGavin lets Sarah and me play tennis, while Leigh and all the other girls have to square dance with the PE boys. I look around for Leigh. I know she has a car today because I saw her pulling into the lot in her mom's old Chrysler, a two-tone two-door.

Sarah and I aren't sixteen yet like Leigh is, even though we're all in the tenth grade, so every day we try to find an older kid with a car to take us off campus for lunch. We've never asked Leigh to take us because you never know when she's going to have her mother's car. Mostly we ask this sweet guy who's a senior in the band, a trombone player, and sometimes we go with this swimmer girl who's a junior with a Bronco. If we ask guys, we always ask guys we would never want to go out with. It would be too humiliating to beg for a ride from a senior on the football team like Trey. But I don't see Leigh anywhere.

I'm late to gym, but I don't mind. I actually prefer it because I hate undressing in front of the other girls. It's not that I'm overweight or ugly or anything. Though I'm cute enough and have blonde hair, I'm shorter and look younger than the others, with smaller hips and breasts. At home, everyone is always covered up. My mother wears a pink or blue cotton nightgown and a pink flowery robe, and my father wears neat Brooks Brothers pajamas with a tattered terry-cloth robe that used to be brick red, but is now pale with spots from too much washing.

Sarah likes undressing in front of other people. When I spend the night at her house, she'll walk down the hall from the bathroom to the bedroom, naked and thin, her straight past-the-shoulders hair hidden under a towel knotted in front, and when I stand there frozen, watching, Sarah says, "What?"

I see Sarah already on the court, sweatpants on, her lucky blue Fila jacket tied around her waist. She's hitting her serve so hard that it bounces in the square, then flies to the metal fence with a clang. My serve takes a couple bounces before it hits the fence with barely a rattle. I can still beat Sarah, though I know it's only a matter of time until she learns to play more consistently, eases up on her power, mixes up her shots. Right now it's a head game—our matches are close, but I always win.

When I was nine, I went the entire summer, at least ten tournaments in all parts of Arkansas, beating my opponents, even Sarah, 6–0, 6–0. I'm so dreamy about the days when I used to kill everyone.

Sarah and I play a groundstroke game to eleven. I win, barely, by hitting the same shot, deep with topspin, every time. I really do get into a kind of rhythm, and I start thinking of myself like a Buddhist monk chanting *one two three hit* or like my father who meditates saying the same secret word over and over.

Afterward, we fill up an empty tennis-ball can with water and take turns drinking and talk about what we're going to do for lunch.

"We could stay here," I kid. "Get a Coke and an ice-cream sandwich and stand outside."

"Ah, Chandler baby, no," Sarah says, and I smile.

We start walking back to get dressed for third period, and I spot Leigh smoking under the stadium bleachers. She's long-limbed and awkward there in the shadows but has a pretty face, her wavy brown hair pulled back by two silver barrettes.

I twirl my racquet twice and catch it on the grip. "Why aren't you inside square dancing?" I ask.

"They don't ever miss me," Leigh says.

"Can I have one of those?" Sarah says, then sets her racquet and the tennis balls on the ground.

"Sure," Leigh says, like she's honored that Sarah would smoke one of her cigarettes, and lights it for her. Sarah and Leigh don't really know each other, only a little about each other through me.

"Hey, Leigh," I say, thinking about my lunch plan, and I take the rubber band out of my hair, letting my ponytail fall. "Did your mom call in sick?"

Leigh doesn't answer, just gives me a look like she's ashamed.

"I don't mean anything by it," I say. "I just wondered if you have the car today?"

"I have the car."

"You're sixteen?" Sarah says.

"Yeah, since October." Leigh pauses a moment, taking a drag and looking at us. "Why, do y'all want to go to lunch?"

I smile. "That'd be great. Thanks, Leigh." I reach out for a smoke, and Leigh lights my cigarette off hers, then flicks hers away.

Sarah lets her hand fall to the side and drops her half-smoked cigarette in the grass. "So, how about Hardscrabble?"

Hardscrabble is the name of the country club where Sarah and I have spent nearly every day of our lives playing tennis. I used to think the name was a golfing term, but my dad told me it's because the golf course used to be a farm, which was known, because of its rocky conditions, as a "hardscrabble" way to make a living. It seems weird to me that it's a name of a place where rich people go to take it easy.

"Definitely," I say. "Hardscrabble."

"Do we have time?" says Leigh.

"I have study hall next period," I say. "I can call in our order. No problem."

"But I'm not a member," Leigh says.

"We know, and we'll buy," Sarah says. "What do you want?"

Leigh gathers her hair in her hand, then lets it go. "Maybe a turkey sandwich. With bacon."

"You mean a *club sandwich?*" Sarah says.

"I guess," says Leigh.

"All right, Leigh," I say. "We'll meet you in the parking lot right when the bell rings. We have to beat everyone out and get there, or we'll never finish in time. It's like a sit-down dinner."

"I know," Leigh says. "We'll get there fast. I'm a good driver."

"Then we'll see you later," Sarah says. She picks up her racquet and the can of balls and walks away, and with the cigarette in one hand and my racquet in the other, I follow.

In study hall, all the football players sit in the back and never study. The closest they come to any real work is copying assignments from me or any other humanitarian who will let them. Trey is always goofing off and thinks it's funny to hold up notes written in big letters that say something like, "Hi, Chandler." I always smile when he does that, even though I know it's subnormal.

Trey and I went to the movies once, and he called my house right before he was supposed to show up and asked my dad, who rarely answers the phone, to ask me if I would iron his shirt for him. My dad was laughing and yelled the message up to my room, and I yelled back that I would. And when Trey came to the door, my dad actually answered because he said he wanted to meet *this* boy. Usually, if I had a date, my dad would run and hide in the kitchen and leave my mother or me to open the door. It's not that my dad doesn't care about who I go out with. He just doesn't know what to say. And neither did Trey and I on our one and only date.

Coach McGavin runs the study hall. What an easy schedule he has—gym and study hall. I walk up to him, and he gives me the pass before I even say what I want it for. "Thanks, Coach," I say. I go to the pay phone and call Hardscrabble's clubhouse, where we like to eat lunch. They also have a snack bar, but it's not nearly as nice as the clubhouse. I order a club sandwich for Leigh and two French dips for Sarah and me. I tell the guy who answers to have it ready at 11:30, that we're coming from school, that we only have forty minutes. He says, "No problem. Last name Carey, right?" I feel a little embarrassed that he knows my voice. I say politely as I can, "That's right. Thanks so much."

Sarah and I meet by the trophy case and walk out to the parking lot together. Leigh is already waiting for us in her mom's car.

"Cool," I say, getting into the backseat.

"Yeah, Leigh," Sarah says and shuts the door. "How'd you get out here so fast?"

"I left physics early."

"You must have Mr. Holbrook," Sarah says. "I have him first period, and I'm always late. He doesn't care."

"Well, we can't be late coming back from lunch," I tell Leigh.

"We have geometry fourth. Mrs. Schneider."

Leigh nods and starts driving. "Want some music?"

"Yeah, baby," Sarah says and starts turning the dial.

We're just about to leave the lot when we hear a horn blaring behind us. We all turn to see Trey hanging halfway out the window of his new black Firebird, his white jersey waving. We take a right and a quick left onto Cliff Drive, the road that

Hardscrabble Country Club is on, and Trey follows us, with his shiny chrome rims, his big tires, his tail fin high in the air.

"God, what a tacky car," I say.

"It's not that bad," Sarah says. "I kind of like it."

"I'd rather be in this one," I say. "Right, Leigh?"

Leigh turns back and smiles at me, then looks ahead, speeding up a little. Cliff Drive is a long, windy road lined with expensive houses with long driveways. It's hard to see the houses from the road, but Leigh keeps glancing back and forth, trying to see something. Sarah rolls down her window and climbs halfway out, the purple streaks in her dark hair blowing, and yells "woo" over to Trey like she's at a concert.

"Good Lord," I say and pull on her to get back in. "Be careful."

"Hey," she says. "Relax."

As we round the corner coming up to the club, I turn around and see Trey taking the curve too fast. His car swings off the road, jackknifes, then goes into a ditch, only his stupid tail fin showing. Sarah sees it, too, and laughs.

"What a moron!" I say.

"What is it?" asks Leigh, and Sarah tells her what she missed.

Leigh slows down and takes the exit for Hardscrabble. She circles the lot, hesitating. "Should we go back?"

"No, he's fine," I say. "He's wrecked there twice before."

"Yeah, don't worry about little Trey, Leigh baby," Sarah says. "Try to park up front."

"Yeah," I say. "Time is of the essence." This is a phrase my mother uses when I'm running late, which is almost always.

We rush into the country club and walk through the bar, and Sarah and I grab nuts and mints from little bowls set around on small marble tables. In the dining room, we sit by a window, so we have a good view of the golf course. Sarah tells Leigh about how I almost killed her with a 7 iron. She always tells that story whenever she gets the chance.

A waiter comes up to us with menus, but I tell him we already ordered by phone, and he smiles and fills our water glasses and takes our drink order. I get a Coke like always, and Sarah gets a virgin strawberry daiquiri, and Leigh orders iced tea.

Leigh leans over and says in a hushed voice, "Is everyone that works here black?"

I shrug. "I guess."

"I think I've seen a few white ones before," Sarah says, then waves her hand and gets a different waiter to bring us crackers and bread and butter.

"This is really nice," Leigh says. "Thanks for bringing me here."

"Thanks for driving us here," Sarah says, buttering a cracker.

The waiter returns with our sandwiches on a big round tray he carries with one hand above his shoulder, and another waiter follows him, like he's the other waiter's waiter, carrying our drinks.

"Cool," I say. "We still have twenty-seven minutes."

On the side of Leigh's plate are silver cups with mayonnaise and mustard, and she spreads both on each layer of the four triangles of her sandwich. Sarah and I dig into our French dips and have a silver cup of ketchup between us for our fries.

"This is way better than the school cafeteria," Leigh says.

"Chandler and I," says Sarah, "have never eaten there. We've successfully gotten a ride every day for three months. And in just four more months, we won't have to. I'm sixteen in March."

"When are you sixteen, Chandler?" Leigh says.

I take a drink of my Coke. "Not until next September."

"God," Leigh says. "I'm almost a year older."

"Chandler's got a bad birthday," Sarah explains, holding her virgin daiquiri like it's real. "If she were just one month younger, she could play sixteen-and-under tennis for an extra year." Sarah waves her drink around. "So Leigh, what's up with your mom?"

Leigh takes a bite of her sandwich, then a drink of her iced tea. "What do you mean?"

I eat a fry and Leigh doesn't say anything, so I say, "Nothing's up with her. She just calls in sick a lot."

"She hates working," Leigh says.

"Man, I don't blame her." Sarah raises her glass and says, "To not ever having to work."

Leigh smiles, and I smile.

"Let's get out of here," I say. "Time is of the essence."

I raise my hand for the waiter, and he brings over our ticket, and I sign my father's name with a short yellow pencil, *Ben L. Carey #379.*

We have about five minutes before the bell rings. What takes the most time is finding a parking place in the school lot. But Leigh tells us not to worry about it and that if we're late getting back, she'll drop us off by the door.

Leigh turns on the radio and switches the dial around and stops on a commercial that we all know by heart, and we say together in a deep, dopey voice, "C&H Tire. 8701 Rogers. Where we do it just for you."

Leigh takes a right onto Cliff Drive, and we only go about ten yards because there's so much traffic. It normally gets a little backed up every day with kids rushing from McDonald's or Wendy's, but this is way worse than usual.

Sarah's in the backseat this time, and she yells up, "What the hell?"

Leigh is quiet, concentrating, moving the car slowly.

"I can't tell," I say. I roll down the window and lean out as far as I can. In the distance, I can see a fire truck and blue police lights. A cop is waving cars around.

Sarah leans up, too, and tries to get a look. "Is that all for Trey?" she says.

"It has to be," Leigh says.

We creep forward, and as we approach the curve, I see Trey's black Firebird still tipped down into the ditch. His shiny chrome rims, his big tires, his tail fin.

"That looks pretty bad," Leigh says.

I feel relieved when I see Trey standing there by a cop. He looks fine. The back of his white jersey is clean around the number and not torn or anything. The cop is probably talking to him about the big away game tonight in Pine Bluff, which is pretty far from Fort Smith, about four hours. I think the football team is supposed to leave right after lunch. Trey's probably worried about missing the bus. "Thank God," I say. "He's okay. He's right there."

Sarah is still leaning up over the seat, but she doesn't say anything.

"That's not him," Leigh says. "That's someone else. Trey's #48."

"She's right," Sarah says.

Leigh inches the car forward, then the policeman directing traffic makes us stop, and we're right next to Trey's car. Leigh shifts into park, and we all look. The front end is crumpled by at least three feet against the side of the ditch. Firemen are working to cut Trey out. The door is open, but his body is wrapped around the steering wheel. His head stuffed between the dash and the windshield. There is blood on his jersey and on his head and in the cracks of the glass.

I look away and notice that people are starting to drive around us and that we're the ones who are holding things up. The policeman knocks on the back of our car and startles us, tells us to get moving. Leigh puts the car in drive, and we proceed. Nobody says anything. Maybe we don't know what to say, or what to think. I look at one of the fancy houses and think that I like my house better. And I like Sarah's house even better than mine. She lives in this long sprawling one on the other side of Hardscrabble, on the back nine of the golf course. Sometimes, when I spend the night over there, we'll sneak out and meet guys.

One night Trey met us there with another football player. I was the one who was supposed to be with Trey, but we still had the same problem talking to each other. We lay down on a green, the short grass more perfect than carpet, and looked at the stars. We never kissed, but he put his arm around me, and his other hand rubbed on my shoulder and on my elbow and on my wrist and on my palm and on each finger. He was the first boy to ever touch me like that, and I never even kissed him.

Traffic is moving almost back to normal. The second lunch has already started, and we see kids breeze by the other way, not knowing what's ahead.

Leigh turns off the radio. Sarah starts crying. Leigh looks over to me, and I look back to her, then put my hand over my eyes. Sarah's breathing is loud and erratic. Leigh turns into the lot.

"You can go ahead and park," I say.

"No, I'll drop you off," she says. "I want to."

She pulls up to the entrance of the school, and I wipe my eyes.

"You sure?" I ask. "We'll wait and walk in with you."

"No, go ahead," she says.

I open my door and get out, then pull the seat forward for Sarah. I grip her arm and steady her until she's standing. I start to thank Leigh for the ride but stop myself. I want to tell her that I'm sorry, that we should've gone back, I should've let her go back, but I don't say anything, just shut the door and watch her drive off, all by herself, looking for a place to park.

Sarah and I walk into the school, and I'm wondering how long it will take to forget this walk. It seems too quiet. There should be a commotion in the halls. Others saw what we saw, but classes have already started, and we are going to be late.